Ruthless Attraction

Arlene Koss

Contents

Chapter 1

The balls of her feet burned as she zig zagged through the crowd, pushing her way forwards forcefully. Grunts and gasps of dissatisfied individuals she failed to avoid went past her unnoticed the same as their faces. Sea of heads that bobbed and dipped occupied her field of vision. More and more people flowed out of buildings onto the streets. It almost felt like fate was against her. It just had to happen in a busy Monday afternoon of all times.

"Stop!" A loud voice boomed through the avenue.Those words were directed towards her and she knew it all too well.

Catherine stole a backward glance at her pursuers. They stood out like a sore thumb with those navy blue uniforms and peaked hats. The crowd willingly parted, allowing the two men to run faster. In her opinion it wasn't fair as some people even tried to stop her instead of letting her run freely, obstructing her way to freedom.

It wasn't her lucky day. Everything went so well, until cops spotted her with a hand in man's pouch. From there things went downhill.

The young woman bent forwards, slipping under an arm that darted out from the crowd right in front of her in a lousy attempt to stop her from escaping. Thank the God for her quickness and sharp wit. Catherine didn't even drop her speed iota, forcing her legs to go faster with every nimble stride. Her mind did quick analysis of her surroundings, directing her body and forcing it into obeyence.

Her grip on the knapsack that mindlessly dangled over her left shoulder never loosened. From time to time she adjusted it, doing it more out of a habit than anything else. After all the content of this bag ensured that she'll have something to eat for the rest of the week, maybe longer if she'll have enough willpower to keep away from McDonalds.

She squeezed past people who thronged around the entrance of metro, rudely shoving them out of her way without even looking apologistic. Her breath came in small spurts as she sprinted down the stone steps, swiftly jumping over the metallic rod of gateway and into the underground corridors that were covered in dirty, white tiles.

Her feet slipped outwards as she took a sharp turn, but she didn't let it stop her. Regaining the speed, she darted forwards with even greater abandon.

"I said freeze!" One of police officers yelled, his voice reverberating through the subway loudly. They were hot on her heels.

Catherines heart drummed against her rib cage rapidly as if it was about to leap out of her mouth. Her eyes frantically searched for a way out only to find none.

Crap, crap, crap!

Suddenly her eyes landed on a passel of people boarding a train. Quickly she changed the direction of her run. The metallic door of the train begun to close, but she didn't halt. Everything seemed to happen in slow emotion as she slipped through the narrow gap right into the train and it's door shut close right in front of the two policemen.

It took her a moment to register what had happened. She had escaped. Only barely, but still...

"Haha..." Catherine let out a genuine laugh, drawing even more attention to herself. Nearly all eyes were on her, most of them holding a suspicious, judgmental look that she couldn't care less about. The young woman looked at the two men, grinning from ear to ear mockingly.

Maybe I shouldn't....Nah, I definitely should.

She raised her middle finger for them to see. The shocked, angered expressions amused her to no end. Oh, it never gets old.

The train begun to move and soon enough the platform with two police officers disappeared from sight. Catherine slumped down in one of free seats besides an old, grumpy looking man that was reading a magazine, being too observed in an article to notice the world around him. In any other time she would've emptied his pockets, but too many watchful eyes were fixed on her now.

She sighed, letting herself relax a little. Her breathing was still unsteady from all the running and droplets of sweat covered her flushed cheeks. Her fingers were starting to cramp up from the vice-like grip she had on her bag that now lied on her lap. First bite of winter was getting her good, cold air came as quite a shock to her throat and lungs and she already caught herself coughing more often.

As the train became more crowded she decided that it was about the time to get out. Also there was this stench of urine that made her want to burry her face in her hoodie, just to prevent the odor from making her sick.

Catherine pulled the grey hood over her head, tucking loose strands of her nut brown hair back. This time she didn't push past the people, going along with the pace set by the crowd around her. She shivered as another gelid breeze blew past her, chilling her to bone. A hoodie and a leather jacket she wore didn't block the cold, making her quiver like a leaf in late Autumn. Winter was a harsh time for someone like her, so she relished every warm day that came around.

Her eyes landed on a signboard that said 'Pawnshop' with big, bold letters. She paused, stopping in front of the shop window where tons of unredeemed, and most likely stolen, items were displayed.

Catherine hesitated before entering the pawnshop. A bell chimed as she sauntered into the shop which could be mistaken for lorn if it wasn't for loud snoring that came from behind the counter. The young woman walked over the dirty floor which was covered in some tawdry carpet. She peeked over the counter, only to see a man in his mid fifties, sprawled in a chair. His head was thrown back and mouth hanged open. It was a surprise he hadn't swallowed a fly, because the place teemed with those.

She cleared her head to get the bold man's attention. Nothing.

"Umm...Excuse me?"

Still no response.

"Wake up!"

The man sprung up in his chair, nearly tipping it over. His eyes darted from one side of the room to another until he finally spotted the young woman standing in front of him.

"What!?" He bawled, enraged that someone woke him up from the slumber. There was a visible pause as his eyes roamed over her figure shamelessly. His expression lit up and attitude changed in blink of an eye. "I mean, how can I help you, young lady?"

Catherine ignored his overly sweet tone, pulling out a watch from her bag. It looked flashy with cold glinting in the light. Maybe it was expensive, maybe some cheap crap, but it looked impressive enough to get her some money.

"I would like to sell this." She put the watch on the counter. The potbellied man stood up from the chair, putting on his glasses and taking the item in his portly hand. He examined it with a look of an expert before setting it down with a huff.

"I can give you 50 dollars. No more."

"What! It's worth at least hundred dollars!" Catherine bargained, motioning towards the watch with her hand as if trying to present it as more valuable.

"No can do, sweetpie. It's the highest price I can offer you, take it or leave." The man said harshly, looking at her almost evilly. "Though, maybe I can give you more if you...give something back." He said with a nasty laugh, his eyes trailing up and down her body. That alone made her face twist in revulsion.

"To hell with that!" She snapped, pushing the watch closer to the man. "I'll take those 50 dollars."

The man scoffed, losing interest in her after the rejection. He took the watch and pushed crumpled 50 dollar bill towards her. Catherine took the money and left the pawnshop apace. She stomped down the street, her eyebrows furrowed in a deep frown. "Disgusting pig...." She murmured under her breath, feeling herself grow more annoyed by every passing second.

She was so busy with her own thoughts that she didn't even notice the upcoming disaster.

Catherine's head snapped up at a sharp sound of tires screeching. Her whole form froze and mind went on a standstill as she watched how a sleek, black car advanced towards her in full speed.

Chapter 2

The shock knocked every wisp of air from her lungs. The color drained from her face and eyes widened in pure terror. Her mind was wiped of any thoughts as she duly followed the movements of stalling car.

It stopped mere inches from her, so close she could particularly feel the vibrations of engine. Her legs shook, knees threatening to buckle. Catherine lied her arms flat on the hood of the car for support. It was the only thing that kept her from collapsing onto the asphalted road. Her whole form begun to shake as her mind processed what fate she had narrowly avoided thanks to dumb luck.

Her stare flickered upwards, meeting eyes so icy they could impale you just by single glance. There was no warmth in them only coldness. For a moment she found herself astonished by the two unblinking orbs.

The man who sat in driver's seat looked like someone out of a movie, but instead of a million dollar smile his lips were pulled in thin line and his square jaw was clenched. Two, perfectly shaped, black eyebrows that matched the color of his well combed hair were arched in a deep frown, creating lines on his forehead. He didn't look older than thirty, but was clearly not her age.

The man shifted in his seat, his hand slipping off the steering wheel onto the handle of door. Catherine followed his every move as he got out from the fancy car. With two wide steps he was already standing short distance away from her, looking at her from above. Literally. He was about six and something feet tall, give or take few inches. With her shorter form she had to tilt her head up to look at his face.

"Luckily for you my car isn't damaged. I could overlook this."

Catherine's jaw dropped open at his arrogant tone of voice. He didn't even bother to look at her for long, being more concerned about his car than a person he almost ran over!

"You son of a-I nearly saw my dead grandmother! But all you care about is some piece of metal!?" She snapped, straightening her form and folding her hands across her chest. Her fiery temper spiked up like wildfire and her mouth move on it's own, spitting out the first knee-jerk response that sprung to mind.

Briefly surprise flashed across his features before it was quickly replaced by a somewhat sly and evil look. "It's your fault for not watching where you go. It wasn't me who crossed the street under the red light." He told her calmly, almost like he was scolding a child.

"What! Well, excuse me! I wasn't the maniac who crossed all the possible speed limits!" Catherine yelled, drawing even more attention to them. A small crowd was beginning to form to watch the two argue whilst still standing in middle of the road.

"Do you expect me to apologize for your stupidity?" His eyes seemed to darken making him appear even more intimidating.

"An apology won't fill my stomach. I want you to pay me for emotional distress you caused." She said confidently, refusing to give up just because of a scary man in a suit thought he was a God.

A deep chuckle rumbled through his chest, not quite making it to his eyes.The man took a step closer, invading her private space. Catherine obdurately fought against the urge to take a step back. Every fiber in her body screamed for her to turn around and run, but she was stuck gazing up at the gorgeous man who was now so close that she could feel the heat from his body and smell his cologne.

"Listen carefully, little girl. Your word against mine means nothing. You should be thanking me for letting you off the hook this easily. Try to gain anything from this and you'll regret it. Take my words for granted." His voice sent uncomfortable shivers down her spine and made the little hair on back of her neck stand. There was something unsettling about the way he threatened her while being calm and collected.

Catherine opened and closed her mouth like a mute fish. Screws in her head gritted against each other, trying to figure a good comeback. But her mind was empty.

His lips that were pulled in thin line parted slightly, letting a throatily humph escape. "Pathetic..." He murmured, giving her one last aggravated look before turning his back to her and making his way to the car.

She was left stunned. Did he just call her pathetic!?

"Hey! I'm not done talking to you, jerk!" Catherine yelled, rage radiating off of her in waves.

The man ignored her, not even sparing a second to look at her. That was the last drop in the already brimming glass. Before her mind could register what she was doing, Catherine marched towards him, her nimble fingers itching to do the deed. Her eyes were fixed on outline of a wallet in his pocket and she couldn't resist the urge.

'I'm only taking the compensation for the distress...It couldn't even be called stealing.'

Just as the man was about to get in his fancy car she darted past him, pickpocketing him before anyone could bat an eye. She could feel the lightweight of money and smooth leather under her fingers as she disappeared into the crowd, once again letting her feet carry her past the high-rise buildings and grey masses of human population.

Catherine ran down several blocks, keeping up a good pace. She didn't risk slowing down in case someone was on her tail, but luckily for her, no one followed. Eventually she slowed down, feeling her energy running low.

The young woman clutched at her torso, leaning against a tall brick wall of some run down building as she tried to catch her breath. Her heart drummed against her breastbone and familiar sharp pain tormented her side. "I'm out of shape..." She murmured under her breath, words bitter on her tongue.

Her eyes traveled down to a wallet she was still holding in one hand. It looked brand new, the black leather almost intact. Inside were more creditcards that she could count along with several 100 dollar bills.

Her lips formed into a cheshire grin in her arrogant triumph. "Benjamin Franklin, my favorite dead person. I'm always glad to see you." Catherine flipped through the banknotes proudly, her keen eyes stopping at what appeared to be a visit card. "Layton Grim..." She read the name written on the card, followed by CEO of Grim Enterprises.

She had heard that name somewhere before, but her mind refused to recall from where she knew it. Catherine shrugged, pocketing the wallet. Whatever, it was none of her business anyway. It's not like she would see him ever again....

With that in mind she returned to her old apartment an hour walk away from the center of city. If she had a car it would most likely take twenty minutes for her to get home, but that really wasn't the option considering her financial situation which could be described only as bankruptcy.

Catherine sighed as she dragged her feet up the flight of stairs. Huffing and painting she finally managed to reach the third floor alive. It wasn't like she was completely out of shape, maybe a little rusty, but the fact that she hadn't eaten anything for two whole days was a serious excuse for lack of energy.

She shuffled through her backpack, her fingers digging their way through various crap to reach her keys. The young woman considered giving up few times. Taking the door down sounded like much easier thing to do than find something in that trashcan of a rucksack.

Her expression lit up as she finally felt something metallic brush against her fingertips. Catherine was about to grab onto the object when her neighbors door flew open, startling her.

'And it's lost again...'

She groaned quietly, looking up at who had disturbed her. In a doorway stood a gaunt and very tall man. His pale cheeks had sunken inwards, accenting dark bags under his tired eyes. From the first glance someone could mistake him for someone who just got out of The Walking Dead. And he definitely isn't Rick Grimes.

"How can I help you...Mr...Mr..." Catherine paused, cursing herself for being so bad at remembering names. There goes her attempt to sound polite...

"Anderson." The old man wheezed, his grating voice echoing through the staircase.

"Right, Mr. Anderson." She finished her sentence as if nothing happened, putting on the most innocent face she could muster. Catherine needed all the luck she could get with that man. He was her landlord and she hadn't payed this month's rent...nor the last month's.

"You have a guest." Mr. Anderson said, his chapped lips parting into a creepy smile. "He was persistent, so I let him in."

Catherine felt her heart sink at his words. A guest? She wasn't expecting anyone. There was only one person she could think of that could be that visitor and if it really was him, then her only choice was to run and move to Argentina with naive hope that he wouldn't follow.

She cleared her throat, forcing a smile. "Who is it?"

"How am I supposed to know." The man grumbled back, turning to walk back in his apartment. "Don't forget to pay the rent. I give you three days before I'll throw you out!" He added before shutting the door with a bang.

"Assh*le" Catherine murmured under her breath, turning her attention to wooden door in front of her that suddenly seemed very similar to gateway to hell. Hesitantly she put her hand on the handle and opened the door, praying to all Gods she knew for the guest to be a lost postman.

What she saw though was anything but that. Her eyes widened, mouth forming in an 'o' shape.

From all the people in the damned world, it just had to be Layton Grim.

Chapter 3

Layton's eyes bore into her with blunt refusal to avert his gaze. His face was devoid of warmth or emotions, even more than before.

Catherine blinked several times as if she was seeing things. But the man who calmly sat on her couch with his hands crossed didn't poof like she had hoped.

The mere seconds she wasted standing in the doorway, gawking, felt like decade. Indistinct sounds was all she could manage in her state of shock. She was expecting someone unpleasant. A police officer or a detective. But not him!

Catherine did the first thing that came in her mind - bolt. Or at least attempted to do so...

The second she swiveled around to run for it, her body collided with a hard wall that had appeared out of blue, making her stumble backwards.

A tall, bald man stared down at her through the hued lenses of his spectacles. To say that he was large would be an understatement. His muscles looked like they would bust out of his suit that tightly hugged his form. The fabric was stretched to its limits. It was surprising that he even managed to squeeze himself in the jacket.

Man's face was about as pliable as a rock. He looked like someone too enormous to move quickly. But he proved that statement wrong.

As if he was capable of reading her thoughts, his hand that stiffly lied at his side shot out like it was remote controlled, and grabbed her by collar. Catherine's hand went to his wrist as she felt her toes no longer touching the ground. Her legs dangled as he held her inches above the floor with no strain.

"Let go of me!" She shouted as he pushed her inside her apartment. Her steps flattered and she barely kept herself for toppling onto the floor. Catherine regained her balance, glaring up at the man who now blocked her exit. There was no getting past him.

Her eyes shifted to the handsome business magnate, once again meeting his pointed gaze. Layton emitted power and confidence, sitting on a couch like a king in a throne.

'Who does he think he is!? First he barges in my home and now his loyal watchdog is jostling me around like a rag doll! All that over few Franklins!'

"Sit." Layton enjoined, motioning towards a chair in front of him.

"I'm not your lap dog to obey command sit."

"Suit yourself." He said with asperity, clearly displeased with her answer. "I'll get to straight the point. Return what you stole." His orotund voice send shivers through her body.

"I don't know what y-"

"Don't play dumb." He interrupted her, eyes narrowing to slits. "You took my wallet, and now you'll return it to me otherwise I'll hand you over to police." Layton growled.

She had to resist an urge to gulp at his threat. He was in control of the situation, pressing the right buttons to make her more agitated. His fierce eyes had her gnawing in the insides of her cheeks as she strived to maintain her cool.

After a good minute of counting cons and pros, she sighed in defeat. Reaching in her pocket she took out his wallet, tossing it towards him.

For her disappointment he caught it effortlessly. She had hoped it would smack his face.

"For my defense, I only took what belonged to me. You refused to give me compensation, so I took it myself." Catherine stated, putting as much confidence in her voice as possible.

"For a moment I thought you weren't quite as dumb. Looks like I was wrong." Layton said matter-of-factly, as if insulting someone was perfectly normal for him.

"Call me stupid if you wish, but at least i'm not a jackass." She snapped, returning his harsh stare with one of her own. "You got what you needed. Take your bossy attitude and get out of my apartment!"

Layton's expression was priceless. It was a mix of astonishment and pure irritation that seemed to be building up with every spoken word. But it lasted only for a fleeting moment. The corner of his pale red lips tugged upwards in a cunning smirk. He looked cocky more than anything and maybe...tad amused.

"You have guts, I'll give you that." He pulled his visit card from his wallet, putting it on a coffee table. "Be in my office at 9am sharp." Layton stood up, straightening his well cut suit jacket of any wrinkles. Completely ignoring the confused look Catherine was giving him, he made his way towards the door.

"W-wait! Why the hell do I have to go to your office! You got all your Franklins back! Our business here is done!" She exclaimed, her mind failing to read what was going on in that man's head.

"This is where you're wrong, Spitfire." Layton turned around to face her as he was about to walk out of the front door. His smirk stretched wider, his cold eyes glimmering like one's of a mischievous child. "Don't be late."

And with that he left, his loyal dog hot on his heels. Catherine was left standing in middle of her living room, her mind a surging perplexity. "What the hell just happened..." She murmured, dumbfounded.

Her eyes lingered on the closed front door for a long while before she looked down at the visit card that lied on the old coffee table. She slumped onto the couch, exact the same spot where Layton sat minutes ago.

The young woman stared at the small piece of firm paper without bothering to feign that she understood what's going on. What could a man like him would want from her?

'I shouldn't go...Who knows what that maniac has in mind! But then again...if I don't go...He could call cops on me. Then what? I'll be arrested and brought to jail! I won't fit in there! Maybe he was joking. What's with the nickname anyway? That's not very original. STOP! Concentrate woman! Think!'

"Grr..." Catherine groaned, running her hands through her hair in frustration.

A phone in her pocket went off, pulling her out from her thoughts. A long sigh escaped her lips when she saw who was calling. The name that popped on the screen alone was enough to make her want to throw the Nokia against the wall. Not that it would break it...She could roll a tank over it and nothing would happen.

"What is it Amanda?" Her tone held annoyance that she didn't put any effort in hiding. She already knew what her favorite colleague wanted.

"Catherine! Thank God you picked up your phone! I tried calling Sasha and Josh, but they wouldn't pick up!" She whined petulantly. "I have a huge request-"

"Let me guess. You want me fill in for you..."

"Yes! How did you know!?"

"Telepathy."Catherine grumbled sarcastically.

"Wow! You really are awesome!" Amanda exclaimed, clearly not getting the joke. "So, can you please take over for me this one last time. Pretty please."

'I understand why Sasha and Josh ignored her calls...'

Catherine rubbed her temples, eyes traveling back to the visit card that had made it's way in her hand without her noticing. "Fine...But only this once." She murmured, ending the call before Amanda could say anything else. Maybe it was for the best. Work always took her mind off of things.

Forcing her legs into obedience she stood up from the comfy couch. She could feel the laziness creep up on her, particularly begging her to curl into a ball and take a cat nap.

Fatigued by all the day's events and hungry, she once again made her way out from her apartment. The second she agreed to Amanda's request, she regretted it. But now it was too late.

By the time she arrived at the old bar downtown, it was already late evening. The sun had gone down, but the life in city had just begun.

Hundreds of conversations told in loud voices, all of them competing with the rock music that dominates the atmosphere filled the cramped space.The crowd was young, students from the university for the most part, all of them getting nearer to being wasted by each emptied glass.

A layer of smoke hung low in the stale air, mixing with odor of alcohol, sweat and sex. At first it made her sick and caused severe headaches, but now it was her accustomed routine.

Catherine winded her way through the warm bodies, tying a black apron around her waist while dodging the arms of drunk, hormonal teenagers. Ignoring the cat calls and wolf whistles that were directed towards her, she finally managed to get to the bar.

A familiar young man was serving alcohol to the customers, goofy smile plastered on his face. He was around her age, but looked much younger due to his boyish features.Though he was pretty handsome anyway with hazelnut brown hair that's always slicked back smoothly and ebony eyes that were similar to one's of a puppy. He was pretty well built as one would expect from a captain of a swimming team, but not too much for it to stand out.

"Hey!" Catherine greeted him with a smile as she came to stand besides him behind the counter.

"Hello stranger!" Nick's smile widened as he saw her, adorable dimples appearing on his smooth cheeks. "Wasn't Amanda's shift tonight?"

"I'm filling in for her."

"Again?" His smile fell, turning into a frown. "Couldn't you turn her down?"

"I could have. But I have things to get off my mind. Laying around wouldn't do me any good." Catherine replied while fetching a drink for a blonde woman who seemed to already have enough of those. But who was she to say no to a paying client?

"Things to take off your mind...huh.." He paused, putting a colorful cocktail on the counter and flashing a young, beautiful woman his famous flirtatious smile. "Enjoy." He said with a wink, before turning his attention back to Catherine. "So, what did you do this time?"

"I didn't do anything!" She said, earning herself a raised eyebrow.

"Liar." Nick tsked. "You can tell bullshit all you like, but ya aren't fooling me. Spill it."

Catherine sighed. Nothing ever slipped past him. Nick's like that in-between the social lines type of guy, he's a social guy to most people. He is a good talker when he can be, but it does get ridiculous when he tries to pun too much. He is a nice guy to just get talk about problems or finding places, he'll even take time off his day to guide people to areas. Nick is determined and confident and someone she could could trust. But in this case she had her doubts.

"Do you know a man named Layton Grim?" She asked after a pause, giving in to his 'I'll-be-a-shoulder-to-cry-on' attitude.

"Are you kidding me? Who doesn't? He is one of richest people around, owns nearly half of the city. Why are you mentioning him all of a sudden?" Nick asked, growing suspicious. Then something in his expression changed as if someone flicked a light switch on. "Don't tell me you got in trouble with him..."

"I guess you could say so..." Catherine mumbled hesitantly, cringing at her own words. "I kinda bumped into him and...took his wallet?" Her sentence trailed off, coming out more like a question than anything else. She half hoped that Nick wouldn't hear her over the loud music, but that wasn't the case judging by his reaction.

"You WHAT!?" All the people in hearing range turned to look at the pair with mix of inquisitiveness and uncertainty.

"Shh! Tone it down!" Catherine panicked, glaring at her friend.

"Why would you do that!?" He yelled in a whisper, barely keeping himself together.

"It was utterly his fault! He nearly ran me over with his fancy ass car! I only took my compensation for distress. I had no idea that he'd show up in my apartment demanding it back!"

"Please tell me you gave him the money..." Nick said, nervously running his hands through his hair, messing it all up. He no longer payed attention to the unsatisfied people who were demanding drinks, concentrating only on her as if his life depended on it.

"I had no choice. He had one of his goons with him!" Catherine said, getting back to work before her boss noticed and got both of them fired. "But now he wants to see me in his office tomorrow morning..."

There was a heavy silence on Nick's part as he observed her carefully, like he was trying to find a card that said 'April's fools' written on her head. "You're so dead..." He said after the awkward pause, his tan skin looking pale. "That man is particularly American Yakuza."

"Great .A mafiozo..." Catherine grumbled. "Thanks for encouraging words. Now there's no way I'll go there now!"

"No,no,no. You have to or else he'll hunt you all the way to Antarctica!"

"I won't go! No one can force me!" She said, jabbing a finger at his toned chest. There was a moment of silences as she considered her words, recalling the scary bodyguard who she faced few hours ago. "Okay...Maybe I'll go. But what could an asshole like him want from me!?"

"I dunno...But in your place I would be worried." Nick added, returning to his work without another word.

'I'm so doomed...'

Chapter 4

A groggy groan rumbled through her throat as she shifted on her other side, her hand ferreting around in desperate search for a warm blanket that she failed to find. Her usually cozy bed also felt different, hard. The billowy pillow was also replaced by something soft and furry that kept tickling her nose. Catherine rolled on her back, trying to make herself more comfortable, but ended up in even more uncomfortable position. With an unsatisfied moan she peeled her heavy eyelids open. God, she was tired.

Sunrays were fighting their way through the pale grey draperies into the room. Beams of light were uninvited and very much unwelcomed, signaling the arrival of morning.

'Morning! What time is it!?'

With novice-like grace she jolted up, nearly tripping over the fury carpet she had passed out on few hours ago when she returned from the nightshift. Her eyes frantically searched for the digital clock nestled on her nightstand. It glowed green with the numbers '08:31' displayed.

"Bollocks!" Catherine shouted, probably loud enough to wake up her neighbors since the walls were near paper-thin.

Of all days to be late, it just had to happen now.

There was no time for shower or breakfast. She didn't even have time to glance in the mirror before leaving. Otherwise she wouldn't have left with her waitress uniform still on, including the black apron. All she managed to do was to grab her leather jacket and pull on her shoes on the way out from her apartment.

Catherine bolted down the stairs and into the streets like an Olympic champion at the start gun. The slapping noise of her sneakers resonated around the vandalised walls of the housing estate with a clanging echo. She quickened her pace to an all out sprint, taking sharp turns left and right until she finally halted when she reached the bus stop.

It was unusually empty. Dreadful feeling came over her. Checking the time she cursed loudly. She was five minutes late for a bus.

"I swear! What else could possibly go wrong!'

She took a moment to regather herself. All her thoughts were abandoned as she once again begun to run. She was nimble and knew the city better than anyone. Maybe, just maybe she stood a chance of making in time. A fervent desire to live was enough to get her leaden feet moving again.

Catherine scampered down the main street, shoving people out of her way as she went. For a second she was running so fast that she thought that a lightening bolt hit her and now she was the Flash.

Yeah, right. Maybe a snail version of him.

Thanks to a miracle she arrived three minutes and twenty four seconds before nine. Gasping and panting for air she dragged her feet up the last steps that leaded to large glass door of a fifty floor building. Her head was spinning and she felt very dizzy. There was this numb feeling in her legs which never lead to anything good. It felt like walking through a mist, everything went by her in a blur of colors.

Somehow she managed to get to the reception desk where a very bored lady sat. It was beyond her to notice anything else besides woman's brunette hair and blue eyes that were now fixed on her. "How can I help you?" The receptionist asked, sounding concerned.

Catherine couldn't make out the question or what was about to follow. At that moment she knew that she was clocking out. Her sight was clouded by black dots that hungrily devoured her field of vision. Then everything went black.

Her eyes flickered open to a brightly lit room as something jarred her up from her unconscious state. From the carousel of random ideas that ran through her head came an order - a subtle awareness of who she was under the flow of thoughts with their loose connections to her surroundings. After a few moments she began to analyze the environment.

First thing she noticed was a man standing behind his desk, his back turned to her. He stood facing the floor to ceiling windows, gazing out at the cloudy, stormy skies, a glass of something clearly liquor in his hand. He wore a business suit, one that was as clean and fit as the highest of class businessmen in the world. Everything about him screamed that he was refined, beyond all measure, that he was immensely powerful.

Even though her foggy mind she could make out who the man was.

"I see you're awake, Miss Cavenon." Layton remarked coldly as he raised the glass to his lips.

Catherine frowned, slowly sitting up in the couch she was laying on. "How very observant of you..." She grumbled, glaring daggers at the arrogant businessman as he turned around to face her. Taking in his angular features and keen eyes that shined with unspoken challenge, she once again came to understand that he was undeniably handsome to the point where it almost seemed inhuman, even one glance at him could make the most modest of girls throw themselves at him. He would be the man any male wanted to become and any girl dreamed to marry. That much she had to admit. But what got her attention more than his looks were the unnerving feeling of danger that made her stomach turn in knots.

"I asked you here for a reason." He said, brushing off her insult. He motioned towards the chair across from him, "Sit." He ordered. His tone showed he would brook no argument, that to defy him now would be punishable, and that there was very little outside authority could do to aid her should she choose to defy him.

"And what would that reason be?" Catherine asked, refusing to move from the couch. Maybe it was foolish to disobey. In fact it could end with her head being served on silver tray. But as witless as it was, there was still some fight left in her. Him commanding her around felt like someone pawing the delicate strings of her nerves and ever so lightly touching the switch that was better be left alone.

"I want to hire you." He turns to her, his expression that of a businessman, bored to tears of a dull applicant, his features shifting rapidly back to the human form she had first witnessed, power, wealth, and monetary prowess screaming from his every pore.

"Wait..What?" Catherine blinked, sure that she heard him wrong. "Is this some kind of prank?" She asked stupidly.

"Does it look like i'm joking, Miss Cavenon?" He asked her coldly.

"I guess not. People like you don't have a sense of humor." She retorted. "But if I remember correctly I didn't apply for a job. Why the hell would you want to hire me!?"

"I found your attitude amusing." He remarked almost casually.

"So you want to hire me because you want me to entertain you?" Her mind was failing to process where this conversation was going.

"I don't have the time to be entertained by you. Momentary amusement perhaps, which, you should have been able to do based on how you act. But I won't be playing cat and mouse with you." Layton's demeanor shifted slightly, he was less serious, less harsh now, but still just as tempered. "You'll work for me because you have the right qualities for this job."

"Wait! I never said I'll agree to work for you!" Catherine interrupted him, standing up from the couch.

'There was no way i'll would work for this egoistic douchebag! He must be sick with his head to even consider this deal!'

"I'll be going now, Mr. Grim." She said, turning on her heel to leave only to be stopped by his thunderous voice.

"You have not been dismissed yet."

Catherine turned around to give him a piece of mind only to freeze on the spot when he approached her slowly, like a shark might approach its prey.

She found herself backing away until her back came in contact with a wall. Even then he didn't stop, closing the distance between them until he was standing directly in front of her. His palms slammed against the wall beside her head, his arms locked into place. He had successfully trapped her, preventing her from leaving.

They were inches apart, staring into each other's eyes. Catherine felt her heartbeat speeding up as she stared up at him, having no other choice.

"You'll work for me, otherwise I'll send you to jail for larceny. It's your choice. Take my offer or...don't..."

She felt her breath hitch. "You don't play fair..."

"I never do." He smirked haughty. "Welcome to your new workplace, Spitfire."

Chapter 5

From his desk in Seattle city, Layton stared at the bounty on his large display, reading over the information for the fifth time that day. He pulled his Intelli-glasses off and shuddered slightly, running his hands down the sides of his face. He stared up at the ceiling of his office and released a long, low groan that could almost have been related to a growl.

It had been a long time since a bounty had been placed on him, though, not so long ago he was tangling with the latest bunch of Vatican based Assassins, they had nearly blown the building he sat in now to pieces. It was only at the last moment his agents had discovered the first of the explosives and a building wide sweep was performed.

Leaning back in his chair, Layton felt it tilt backwards as he studied the visually perfect metal that made up the box he spent his working days in when he was filing paperwork. His acute vision could see the tiny imperfections, the atomic structure of the ceiling, and the heat that displayed itself on the atomic level. He rapidly found himself lost in gazing at the metals structure, his mind calculating its density and what it could be melted down into to create something besides just a simple metal plate in his ceiling.

He was jostled from his thoughts a moment later when his sister appeared on his desk with a crack of breaking reality. She lounged upon it in a pseudo-sexual pose that would seduce most men of his position into ravishing her upon the desk, and her body was one that could stand it. She was a vision of beauty, her form wasn't slender necessarily, but she had curves in all the places that drew the eye, and in her current attire, a very revealing ladies business suit, she could draw nearly anyone's eyes.

She stared at him for a long moment before the raised brow on his face brought her back to her senses. She smiled lightly, and sat up, to the edge of the desk, not upsetting a single file, or folder that was stacked neatly on the end, not disturbing his computer interface, or knocking over the pen-well that sit beside his interface. As she sat beside the files, she didn't even seem to displace the desk's surface.

"Vanity..." He began.

She shook her head, and scrunched up her face, "Lunchtime. You haven't eaten in fifteen hours." she interrupted him.

"Since when are you the caring sister?" Layton released a sigh.

"Have no mistake, I'm not." She spoke, her tone holding a dark tint to it. "I heard you have a new toy. I thought humans weren't worth the time these days. Too short lived and fragile." She spoke, repeating what he had once said. "Is it her soul?"

Layton frowned deeply, his hands forming into a fist. "Is that why you're here?"

"Not quite." His sister, Victoria as humans call her, spoke, flipping through some restaurant's menu. "I think I'll have Coq au Vin. I would prefer a young man's soul, but I guess I'll have to wait until next action. Speaking of witch, Lust already set a date. 21st of December. Will you attend?"

"I will." Layton rumbled, turning in his seat he stared out at the Seattle skyline. "Is that all?"

"What do you plan to do with her?"

"With who?"

"That girl. If you just wanted her soul, you would've taken it by now without hiring her. What's so special about her?" She interrogated.

"It's none of your business, Vanity." His voice held power to it and eyes flashed golden, fleetingly showing his true, sinister nature.

A feminine chuckle echoed through his office. "Have fun with her Avarice...Just don't get carried away." She winked, elegantly standing up from where she was sitting on his desk and leaving his office. Layton watched her go in reflection on the windows, half smile making its way to his lips.

That human girl was part of his game, just another thing to erase the boredom. If she didn't meet his expectations....he would take her soul. She wasn't anyone special, a mere entertainment, that's all.

Chapter 6

"That ASSHOLE!"

"W-wait! Catherine! Don't throw that!" Nick yelled, grabbing onto her arm just as she was about to smash another glass against the nearest wall. Managing to take the brittle item from her iron grip he sighed with relief. A bit too soon.

Smash.

One more glass met with it's inevitable fate.

"He blackmailed me!" Catherine roared, hands clenched in tight fists. Her temper was a wild storm to be endured and now she let it pour down over Nick's head. He could only watch his friend vandalize his kitchen helplessly.

"Please calm down." He tried to speak some sense into her. But it was useless.

"That d*ck! Look what he made me wear!" She motioned to her outfit which consisted of plain white blouse and pencil skirt that reached to just above her knees. When she returned from his office the attire lied on her bed with a note that said: Your style is not suitable for your position. Wear this tomorrow for work.

"I admit it doesn't look like you. But at least you look good." Nick noted, letting his eyes roam her body.

"Stop eye-raping me." Catherine hissed, earning a chuckle from him. "Sorry, sorry. But i'm just glad this didn't end with you six feet under. You know that this is much better than what could've happened."

"I guess so..." She murmured under his breath. It still confused her of why he wanted her as his personal assistant. Of all the people who were ready to kill for the position, he picked a girl that stole his wallet.

"Try to look from the bright side. This job is much better than the one you have and the pay is good. More than good." Nick leaned against the doorframe, crossing his muscular arms over his broad chest as he contemplating the spirited woman. "Besides, isn't this the chance you've been looking for?"

"Why are you always the damn optimist? I don't want to work for him! You do have a point about the money, but I can't drop the feeling that he's plotting something." Catherine grumbled, pacing back and forth. "That man wouldn't hire me otherwise...there is something off about him."

"It's not unusual for men to hire their female workers because of a pretty face."

"Is that supposed to make me feel better!?"

Nick rubbed his temples tiredly. Having to deal with all her tantrums was slowly getting to him. "Then maybe you should make him fire you." He blurt out without thinking.

Catherine stopped her furious pacing. "That's actually a good idea." Her face lit up. If it was a cartoon there would be a light bulb hanging above her head.

"Oh no..." Nick stiffened, realizing what he's done. "That's a very bad idea. Don't-"

"You're genius. I'll make it so he wants to fire me! He made the decision to force me into working for him, so I'll make him regret it!"

"Wait-"

"Thank you, Nick!" Catherine kissed his cheek softly as she walked out from the kitchen, master plan in mind. "See ya later!"

"This is going to end bad..." He murmured under his breath as he watched his friend bolt out of his apartment.

Catherine let her mind wander to all the things she could do to upset her new boss as she made her way to the office. Maybe a little of purgen drug in his morning coffee would do the trick. It for sure would have him glued to the lavatory for a while. But maybe that's a little too harsh. Though his ego could use of some public humiliation.

She marched inside the building with confidence, this time blending in with her surroundings. Well, almost. She was hobbling down the corridors in ten inch heels like a newborn fawn trying to stand for the first time. Catherine constantly found herself repeating the same sentence.

'Don't trip and break your neck!'

By the time she reached the top floor her patience had ran out completely. "Who the hell created these things..." She grumbled for the thousandth time that minute. Her feet ached and the floor felt like it was made of ice and she would slip any moment. It was beyond her to understand how other women manage to look graceful while going through such torment.

Catherine stole a glance around, making sure no one payed attention to her as she kicked off her shoes and left them laying on the floor under someone's work desk that was located in front of Layton's private office. A satisfied sigh escaped her lips as she felt cold tiles against her sore feet, calming the searing sensation. It felt so good that she could particularly hear angels singing in heavens.

"You're late!" A high-pitched voice pulled her out from her thoughts. Looking over she saw a girl with platinum blonde hair that were pulled back in low pony-tail rushing towards her. She was wearing rather revealing blouse and skirt tad shorter than would be considered suitable for office. "Mr. Grim is waiting for his coffee for whole five minutes! You should've arrived earlier!" The woman scolded, scowling at her.

Catherine looked up at clock on the opposite wall. It was 8.45. "I'm not late for anything." She stated dryly, but the blonde ignored her.

"Bring him his coffee!" She yelled, pushing a tray she was carrying in her hands. "Make sure not to spill it or he'll fire you." It was more a threat than a friendly warning. The woman gave her one last reproachful look before continuing her way down the hallway in quick pace.

"What a bitch..." Catherine shook her head, looking down at the cup of black coffee that was placed on a tray. She bit the edge of a smile when an idea came to her head. A plan was hatching, a beautiful plan. It was worth giving a shot.

Her attempt to keep her creeping grin at bay was in vain, but she managed not to laugh out loud. Letting out a breath, she entered Layton's office.

He sat behind his desk, staring at computers screen with creased eyebrows. Layton didn't spare a glance at her as she came in, continuing to glare daggers at his laptop. "You're late." His voice rumbled with clear dissatisfaction.

"Why do I keep hearing that despite the fact that i'm not late." Catherine retorted.

Layton let his eyes roll to the woman in front of him. He merely glanced her over, but she could feel the heat of his stare on her. A cold fire that burned her to bone and paralyzed her thoughts. Again, there was this dreadful feeling in pit her stomach. "You look good in clothes I picked for you." He commented, letting his gaze drop to her bare feet. "What happened to your shoes?" He raised an eyebrow in slight amusement which mixed with an emotion she couldn't quite put her finger on.

"If you mean those Spanish boots, I lost them."

"Then I suggest you to find them, they were expensive." Layton gave her a bored look, not impressed by her answer one bit as if he was expecting something more entertaining. "What are you standing around for? Bring me my coffee already." He said in bossy manner. Catherine had to bite her tongue not to snap at him.

She fought a smile that threatened to show, carrying the salver towards her target. Her eyes sparkled mischievously, giving away that she up to no good. Her high school math teacher had once said that her exuberance for trouble was a contagion. Maybe so, but at least she knew how to have fun and get on others nerves when they deserved it...or she just felt like it.

The urge to do it overrode nagging doubt and as soon as she was standing besides him, Catherine tilted the tray to the side and let the coffee spill all over his perfectly white dress shirt.

As the hot drink came in contact with his skin Layton shot up from his chair. "Fuck!" He yelled, pulling the drenched fabric away from his chest.

"Oh! I'm so sorry! Aren't I clumsy today!?" Catherine snickered, quickly covering her mouth as she released her mistake.

His glare that now was fixed on her took away the glory of her victory (of sorts). She visibly wilted before his first clipped word was uttered. With that look alone she could feel the temperature around them drop for few degrees.

"You did it on purpose." His dominating voice boomed through the office. "That was a very foolish move, spitfire." There was something menacing about his tone that send uncomfortable shivers down her spine.

"What are you doing?" Catherine barely kept herself from stuttering as he slowly begun to unbutton his shirt, exposing his toned chest and six pack. He had a body of a Greek God and face that could make anyone stop in their tracks to stare at him, but his eyes were sharp like two blades. He never once looked away from her as he proceeded to take off his shirt and toss it on his leather chair.

"I think we're both aware of what i'm doing. Or could it be that you're really that ignorant?"

"Is that really the best thing you can come up with!? If you want to insult me at least come up with something more original!" Catherine fired back, her confidence returning with spark of anger.

It was a mistake.

In blink of an eye Layton was in front of her, towering over her shorter form like wall of heat and muscle. His broad chest filled her field of vision, leaving no place for anything else. He grabbed her chin, forcefully tiling her head upwards so she was staring straight into his eyes. The grip was bruising and for a moment she thought she could kiss all her bones goodbye, but his expression was one of implicit composure.

Her eyes widened slightly at his next words.

"I could just kiss you to shut that mouth of yours..."

Chapter 7

"No...no no no no no!" Her back had begun to ache from how it was arched like a bow with her attempting to lean as far away from Layton as possible. Every inch she moved back, he moved in. The predatory eyes never left her own. He didn't even budge when she pushed at his broad chest with her hands.

"Get off of me!" Catherine demanded, sounding anything but convincing. Her heart raced a mile a minute. But even then she refused to avert her gaze.

"Do you hear me-"

Layton caught her hand before she could shove his face away from hers. Effortlessly he forced it down, pinning her against the table. "Do not mess with me, spitfire." His hot breath fanned across her face. Their bodies were close enough for her to feel the warmth radiating off of him in waves.

"Do you really take me for a fool?" Layton's low growl echoed through her head over and over again as his grip on her chin tightened. "Or are you really that short-witted and already forgot who holds the power here? I thought I made it clear. I'm not going to play cat and mouse with you."

His cold eyes bore into her flesh and right through her soul. It was almost as if her feet and hands had turned into numb stones. Her own body had betrayed her, making her unable to move an inch.

"I-im-"

Suddenly there was a knock on the door. A young man in his early twenties peeked his head inside the office. "I'm so sorry, sir! I didn't mean to interrupt!" Clearly what he saw wasn't what he had intended on seeing. The man's voice was way more high pitched than it should've been.

Nevertheless, Catherine couldn't help the relief. Layton's attention finally shifted from her to the door. "What did you want, Dolson?" His voice still held the stern gruffness as he addressed what Catherine assumed would be one of his employees.

"The meeting with partners is about to start, sir." The man spoke, his eyes cast downwards and ears tinted in red color.

"Good," Layton finally begun to loosen his hold on Catherine's hand. "Get me a new shirt and tell Angelique to prepare me a new cup of coffee."

He slipped back into full on business mode. The young woman didn't need a better excuse to slip away from him. Layton didn't bother to hold her either. Though his eyes did capture hers for a moment longer.

"As for you, find the shoes," His perfectly shaped muscles flexed as he sat back down on the leather chair and settled his elbows onto the desk. "Dolson will show you to your desk. You're Dismissed."

The second the large door shut behind her, Catherine released a long breath she didn't realize she was holding. "Fucking hell...Is he always like that?"

"Unless you're a bikini model, yeah...pretty much." The same sandy haired guy answered, offering her a sympathetic look. "Don't mind him. You'll get used to it eventually...Oh and my name is Jeremy Dolson, sorry if I came off rude for not introducing myself earlier."

Catherine looked down at the hand offered for her to shake, getting rid of the thought of voicing the comment that had formed on the ip of her tongue. "Catherine...You can just call me Cat." She finally shook his hand, mastering the friendliest smile she could after everything that had happened a couple minutes ago.

"Cat it is," Jeremy returned her forced smile with a genuine one. "So, you're the new employee?"

"Not by choice, but yeah...I suppose I am now." Catherine grumbled, disregarding the confused look that had crossed the man's face. "Weren't you supposed to get the coffee and that shirt?"

"Crap! I forgot!" Jeremy panicked. "You stay right here! I'll be right back!"

She could swear she saw a cloud of dust raise from the squeaky clean floor with how fast Jeremy disappeared around the corner.

"Everyone's so damn afraid of him..." She murmured, casually sauntering along the tiled floor to find her shoes. If he decided to charge her for losing them, she was sure she wouldn't manage to get much out from her paycheck. The thought alone of how much they could cost send uncomfortable shivers down her spine.

Catherine rounded the corner where she knew she had left the pair of torture devices, coming to an abrupt stop when she saw a tall woman with curly brown hair holding up her one shoe in between her slender fingers.

She was a vision of beauty with her piercing green eyes and curvy yet slim figure. Yet somehow Catherine got the same uncomfortable feeling she got when being near Layton. The said green orbs landed on her. There was something predatory about the woman as she looked her up and down.

"Are these yours?" Her melodic voice was filled with amusement as she swung the shoe back and forth on her finger.

"Yes." Catherine replied curtly, making the woman chuckle.

"Judging by the style, my brother gave them to you. Right?"

"Depends on who is your brother." Catherine once again struggled to keep her stance as the woman approached.

"You work here, but don't know what your supervisors are. What a little lost lamb you are." There was a mock in her voice to which the other woman didn't respond quite well. Instantly her expression became one of anger, but before she could defend herself, the woman spoke again. "You know, Layton Grim. I'm his sister, Ven-I mean Victoria Grim."

It should've been more shocking that the female in front of her was the sister of the big bad CEO himself. But somehow it wasn't. When she looked closely, she could see similarities.

The good looks must be in their blood or something...

Catherine mused idly as she took the shoe from Victoria's finger. "I see." She failed to sound interested in any of it which didn't slip past the slightly older woman.

"You're quite interesting. I'm starting to see what my brother saw in you." Victoria leaned in, startling Catherine by how close she suddenly was to her face.

Did she just sniff me!?

Catherine was sure her expression screamed; WTF! She nearly went stumbling back. The clumsy jerk of her body must've been something funny as Victoria released a hearty laugh, somehow managing to even make that look elegant.

Nick used to tell Catherine that she looked and sounded like a horse when laughing. Needless to say, she never truly cared. Those kinds of conversations always ended with the both of them on the ground, laughing their assess off whilst trying to wrestle each other.

Yes, yes...They were kids at heart.

"What the fuck was that about!?" Catherine snapped, no longer bothering to be polite, even if she hadn't been much of that before either.

"Never mind me. I was just wondering what perfume that is." Victoria's smile was unsettling, anything but friendly. She was like a shark that had smelled blood. "It smells...delicious."

Everything she said gave Catherine creeps. At the moment she didn't even think as far that she wasn't wearing a perfume in the first place.

The awkward exchange was interrupted by hurried footsteps. Moments later Jeremy emerged from the maze of hallways, looking worried.

"Ah! There you are!" His expression relaxed as his baby blue eyes landed on Catherine. "I was looking for y- Miss Grim! Shouldn't you be at the meeting!?" His tone of voice changed again as he addressed the woman. Suddenly the friendly man sounded that much more nervous and serious.

"I was on my way there, but then I found this." Victoria motioned to the shoe that Catherine was holding. "Have no worries, Jeremy, I'm leaving now. Please tell my brother that he has to hurry up unless he want to upset the investors." The smile never disappeared from her face as she begun to head towards whatever business she had.

"Take care, little lamb." She tapped Catherine's shoulder lightly, leaving her with chills.

Those two really are siblings...

"I see you've met Miss Grim. She's one of the partners here, even if the company is ran by Mr. Grim." Jeremy explained, sending Catherine spiralling back from her thoughts.

"Hm.." She simply nodded with her head, picking up the other shoe that still was at the table.

"Come on. I'll guide you to your desk. There's quite a bit of paperwork for you to arrange already." Jeremy gestured for her to follow him.

Catherine watched his back, a bitter thought lingering in her mind.

This is it. Now I really am Mr. Grim's personal assistant.....Fuck.

Chapter 8

T he only sound that filled the narrow room that was her 'office' was of her fingers impatiently drumming against the wooden desk. Catherine had been staring at the painfully slow moving clock for about an hour now. It was exactly 10.30 pm.

A personal assistant isn't supposed to leave work until her supervisor does. He might need you for something any moment, so keep your phone close and the sound always on.

Angelique's, or blonde bimbo's - how Catherine had begun to call Layton's secretary, words echoed through her head over and over again.

"This must be some kind of joke..." She grumbled, glaring daggers at the long needle in the clock that moved yet again.

I'm rotting here alive! How can somebody work for so long!?

All day long she had been dragged back and forth across the office to do various useless tasks such as bringing coffee, getting a tissue or making thousands of copies of some random documents. As if that wasn't all, she was forced to work with Angelique who just happened to be just as annoying as the rest of the workers. And now after all that and constant staring at computer screen she was forced to stay longer because somebody didn't know when to give it a rest!

The chair screeched loudly as she stood up. The deathly looking sharp heels dug into the hard ground as she marched across the tiled floor towards Layton's office. Over the course of day she had mastered the skill of not tripping after every five steps.

Not that she could compete with other women who worked at the office. They were all strangely good looking and their feet never seemed to actually touch the ground when they walked.

Bang!

The door to Layton's office flew open as she stormed inside with a furious look plastered on her face.

"Workday is over!"

"It will be over when I say so and not a second earlier." The cold eyes pinned her down from underneath the thinly rimmed glasses the second she took a step inside the 'Forbidden territory'. "And next time, knock."

"You really don't give a shit about the lives of other people, do you?" She could feel her blood begin to simmer. He didn't even pretend to care for his employees. Just earlier that day she had heard a rumor of him firing his previous assistant for taking a vacation to care for her sick baby. It was something about company investing money in somebody who wasn't even in the office. "I have another job you know! My shift started an hour ago!"

Annoyance made itself present on the man's face. Layton once again glanced up from his glowing computer screen with a look that nearly screamed that she was being a bother. "I do not concern myself with lives of unimportant individuals. It would be a huge waste of my time. As for your other job, It's already taken care of."

"What do you mean?"

"I arranged your dismissal."

"You WHAT!?"

It felt like her entire world had been flipped upside down. The news sent her mind into frenzy whilst the bossy asshole didn't even blink. In fact, he almost looked like he was enjoying how panicked Catherine was.

That sadist pig!

"You can't just do that!"

"I already did." His eyes casually traveled back to papers lied in front of him. "You represent the name of Grim Enterprises now. I can't have my personal assistant working at a nightclub."

"I never asked to be your assistant-"

"This conversation is over. If you have nothing to do, you can make copies of these." A file was tossed forwards without a cast of glance.

"No it's not!" Disregarding the painful thought of her not having a say in this, Catherine stomped forwards, her hands balled into taunt fists. She had every intent on burying her knuckles deep into his sharp jawline. There was no stopping the current of curse words that were threatening to pour over her lips. Her fingers uncurled only for the brief second it took for her to catch Layton's silky tie. The expensive material was stretched to its limits as she tugged at his neck, making his attention rapidly snap back to her.

"Now listen here, you filthy rich bastard! I am not one of your pawns that you can do whatever the fuck you want with! I do not belong to you and never will. Quit messing with my life!"

Silence overwhelmed the office. It was far off from being called comfortable. The Nordic sea hued orbs bore into her, burning straight through her soul. The intensity made the air thicken around them. Catherine felt her heartbeat pick up, a pinch of regret slowly but surely sneaking into her consciousness.

But it was already too late.

A hand shot out to grab a hold of her own. Powerful fingers enclosed around her thin wrist. With a single pull she was sprawled across the desk. Everything in her way was knocked over to roll onto the ground, her pride included. The edge of the desk dug into her ribs painfully as she was once again positioned directly in front of him for the second time that day.

"Do not talk to me like that ever again," The grip on her wrist tightened. "Try to remember what'll happen if you lose this job." A cool smile tilted his lips upwards. "You're such an ignorant woman, thinking that I have no control over you. You are my pawn, and for as long as I say, you do belong to me. Is that understood? Or do you wish to be behind bars for the rest of your pathetic life?"

A lump formed in the back of her throat. Catherine felt small and powerless, even if she still tried to keep on a brave face. His eyes, voice...everything about him made her want to stick her tail between her legs.

"Fuck you."

Layton's narrowed eyes briefly widened. Clearly his warning had been serious enough, but even then she still kept defying him. The scowl was quick to return. Catherine winced as his fingers dug into her flesh. His other hand once again captured her chin.

"I could do that to you."

"Then it would be rape."

"No. It would be your word against mine. And your word means nothing." His thumb lightly caressed her bottom lip before he pulled away altogether, nearly sending Catherine falling onto the ground. "Now get out of my office. Playtime is over."

Layton gave out a tired sigh. His attention once again shifted to the computer screen. His ability to disregard the struggling woman on his desk was almost admirable.

Catherine shimmied off of the table in hurry, grabbing anything she could to maintain her balance, even if the dignity was completely lost. "You better not dare to touch me!"

"Quit flapping your gums. I won't. I do not fuck women who do not want it. Besides, you're not attractive enough to get anyone's attention, not to mention mine."

"You're not right in the head!"

"Humph."

"Don't humph me-" She was suddenly cut off my lights flickering. It was one of those times you got creeps from watching horror movies. Even if they messed you up, you never quit watching.

Screech.

The little hair on the back of her neck stood up at the high pitched screech of metal grinding against metal. Suddenly all thoughts of Layton's threats went flying out of the window. Her head whipped around to look at the office door.

Screech screech.

The sounds were growing louder.

"W-what is that?"

"Be quiet."

Layton had stood up from his leather chair, unreadable look placed on his face. But even through that well sported poker face, she could tell that he was on guard. His eyes spelled danger.

Screeeeech!

Catherine's breath hitched. She was sure the two of them had been the last people in the office. And yet there was a clear thump of footsteps coming down the hallway.

Chapter 9

"Get in the closet."

Catherine glanced over her shoulder at Layton. His jacket had left his broad shoulders to rest on the back of his chair and a finger worked its way to loosen his tie. In any other situation she would've found it hot....and a part of her did even in this one. But the creepy screeching occupied her mind way more than any lewd thought ever could.

"Why-"

"Don't ask questions, just do it." The demand left no place for questions. Anyone at their right mind would obey without a second of hesitation. Everyone that wasn't Catherine.

"I won't get into that closet." Her nose scrunched up at the thought of being stuffed into a narrow dark place along with Layton's coats and whatever else crap he kept there. She was no box to be put away when not needed!

"Why do you have to be so damn stubborn?" Layton glanced at the stiffened figure of his assistant with a flustered look she had never seen on him before.

"Like you're one to talk. I won't get into that closet, kapeesh?!"

"You're being a nuisance."

"And you're being a butt-"

Screech!

What the fuck is out there!?

All thoughts that had been causing her a great headache with how they billowed in her head quieted down at the sound of someone stopping just outside the office door. For all she knew, it could've been anyone, but her gut feeling told her otherwise and that's one thing that had never betrayed her.

Suddenly the door flew open, slamming into the wall with enough force to create a handle size hole. It all happened in blink of an eye. The figure clad in black swished across the office, something long and shiney grasped in its one hand.

There was flash of meal directed towards her and she would've sworn there was also a set of teeth showing beneath the lips that were parted in an insane smile.

Catherine drew in a deep breath. It felt like her last one. And it would've been if a strong arm hadn't wrapped around her from behind. Her frozen body was swiveled around and her cheek ended up pressed right up against broad chest.

A familiar scent of expensive cologne hit her nose. It was all she could recognize at that moment and clung to it for her dear life. The rest was lost in chaos caused by the owner of the creepy smile. It never left her mind, even at state of panicked daze that a pained moan made her snap out of.

Catherine lifted her head from the superbly ironed dress shirt. Layton's expression was twisted in pain. But even then his pale blue eyes never left hers. He seemed almost relieved.

It was a fleeting moment that the emotion lingered before disappearing back behind the veil of his cold temper.

There was not much time to dwell on it either as the next moment she was pushed away like a rag doll, nearling ending up toppling onto the floor like a clumsy toddler. She just barely managed to break the fall by grabbing onto the closest piece of furniture in her way.

Her attention didn't remain on anything for too long these days. But the intruder had all of her attention even when she was balancing on her one leg. That and the red substance that covered her hand from having to cling onto the her boss.

The sticky dark liquid coated her fingers, dribbling down her arm. The blood wasn't hers. It soaked through Layton's white shirt, oozing out of a large thin cut that had formed on his back.

Her brain registred what had just happened embarrassingly slowly. It was only when it became clear that the shiny thing in strangers hand had been a sword, it occurred to her just how dangerous the situation was in first place.

Layton stood leaning against his desk, glaring at the willowy man or woman standing in front of him. The attackers face was covered aside from the mouth that had curved into a nasty smirk.

"I am the punishment of God. He, the great Lord, knows of your sins, and has sent me to send you to your fate." The voice was twisted, higher pitched than anyone would've pictured it to be.

Catherine could only stand frozen as the attacker announced his master plan and raised his sword for yet another blow. Her entire body was tense as she prepared to jump to the gun. It was pure instinct. And perhaps she had a deathwish, but she sure as hell wouldn't be the one to stand by as somebody is stabbed to their death.

That was until an arrogant 'humph' interfered her attempt at being heroic.

"You're nothing." Layton stated, staring at the assassin like he or she was just a fly that would be crashed by a newspaper any moment. "And you will be nothing more than you are right now. Pathetic." There wasn't a hint of worry in his voice as he stood straight.

"You will pay amands,Greed!"

Catherine felt her breath glitch at the sight of blade coming down at Layton. The time moved oddly. At one second it felt like decade had passed in a second and in another it was the other way around. Now time stopped completely.

Her eyes widened as Layton's hand wrapped around the sharp edge of the metal, bringing it to an abrupt halt mere inches away from his neck. More blood begun to seethe from his palm, but he didn't even react to it.

"Whoever sent a sinner to kill a sin, was a fool to make such decision."

Layton's hand grabbed the attacker's neck in a swift movement, much like he had done with the sword.

"Gha!"

The audible crack that echoed through the office was deafening. The sound echoed through her ears over and over again as she watched the body go limp and stranger's neck tilt backwards in an odd angle.

The lash noise made by the person send shivers down her spine. He..or she...was dead. Layton Grim, the man she was forced to work for had just killed someone right in front of her eyes and didn't even care. Or at least appeared not to.

Layton simply dropped the body onto the ground, mindlessly stepping over it to wipe his hands in a clean rag.

Catherine had forgot how to breathe, not to mention talk as she watched him grumbling under his breath about weak mortals trying to kill a someone like him again. He didn't even refer to himself as a human being!!!

"Wh...what..." Her eyes were glued on the body. The word she somehow managed to force past her dry vocal cords were muffled by a loud scream. She didn't even realize that it was her screaming until Layton shot her a warning look.

"You just KILLED that man! KILLED!" She tugged on her hair in distress, making them even more messier than they were before.

"He tried to kill me." Layton responded with a shrug that only ticked her off more.

"You should've called fucking police! You just killed a man! You murdered someone! Fu- No! I'll call the police!" Her words came out in stutter and her hands shook as if she had been attached to electricity.

"No you won't."

A bloody hand stopped her before she could grab the phone off the table.

"Let go of me, you murderer!"

"Quit yelling like an idiot." Layton's grim tightened, making her shake harder. Even if she managed to look him dead in the eye, she was sure her fear was so obvious he could smell it. She almost expected him to mock her for that, but instead his expression remained one of a stone.

"Calm yourself. You won't remember anything in the morning anyway."

"What!?"

Before she could question any further, Layton rested both of his hands on her cheeks. His thumbs stroked lightly along her cheekbones in almost soothing manner.

"You won't remember what happened tonight," His voice suddenly seemed far away. The blue of his eyes begun to change their color to bright golden hue. "You will only know of the events before you entered this office."

Catherine's consciousness begun to slip away. No matter how hard she tried to concentrate on grasping the last bits of control, it was as elusive as air and soon enough the battle was lost.

Her eyes dropped close and body relaxed. The last thing she knew was a pair of strong arms lifting her from the ground.

Chapter 10

"What did I do wrong!? What did I do to deserve this!?" A voice echoed through the endless darkness. It sounded far away, but it was far too familiar to be disregarded or remain unheard.

"You did the right thing, for the wrong man. You should've been smarter than this, girl. Now you owe him, and he'll hunt you down no matter where you go." Another voice responded, a much deeper one, sending chills down her spine.

"I'll run-"

"You cannot escape."

"But I will!"

"You're being naive. There's no getting away from fire in a burning house. Either you let it burn you or you become fire yourself."

Ring! Ring!

"Uhm..." A groggy groan rumbled through her chest, followed by a dissatisfied mumble when annoying blaring of her phone echoed through her single room apartment. As far as she knew it was Sunday. Who would disturb a sleeping person on a Sunday? Or perhaps it was Monday. Either way she couldn't care less. Her head felt like it weighed a ton and her body ached in odd places. Whatever she was doing the night before, she was quite sure it must've somehow ended with at least ten shots.

A hand reached from underneath covers, first slamming against the corner of her nightstand and then finally catching a hold of her very irritating phone. The hand disappeared back under the blanket, a bird nest of brown hair appearing in its place.

"What...." Damn, she sounded like a cat with its tail stuck in a doorway. Her voice could barely be recognizable as human's.

"Don't tell me you're still asleep, Miss Cavenon." Layton's irritated voice boomed from the other end.

"Who the-Oh...."

Right. I'm supposed to be a personal assistant now.

"Don't give me that. The flight leaves in ten, you better get your ass into a car. If you're late, the consequences are on you."

"Wait, what car!?"

Beep, beep,beep.

That asshole hung up on me!

The blanket flew off of her in a swift movement as she hurriedly got up from the warm comfort of her bed. A part of her was really tempted to ignore Layton and sleep some more, but then again, she didn't exactly wish to be woken up by police knocking at her door.

Grumbling under her breath, she scurried around her apartment, picking up whatever clothes she could find. The drowsiness got folks dead, fast, as she once again set off from her apartment in hurry.

The old rusty door of the apartment building nearly flew out of hinges as she made a move to make a mad dash down the street. That was until she was stopped by a well dressed man in his late thirties. He stood near a black Mercedes, waiting for what seemed to be her judging by the look on his face.

"Are you Miss Cavenon?" His voice remained calm as he gave her a once over. He had this judgmental air about him that she already found herself disliking. He reminded her of one of her teachers back at high school. Even man's face was similar to the one stuck forever in her memories.

"Depends on who asks."

"Mr. Grim is expecting you. Please get into the car." The driver explained calmly, already making a move to get into the driver's seat.

"Where exactly are we going?" Catherine had to stop herself from commenting on how the driver was almost as conceited as the CEO of the company itself.

"To the airport. The plain leaves for New York shortly."

That was all the man bothered to tell her before setting the car moving along the Seattle streets.

New York!?

She couldn't remember anyone telling her anything about some trip to New York. But now that she thought about it, she also had zero memories of what had happened yesterday evening as well. The last thing she remembered was cursing her boss for making her stay at work for so long. And then the picture went black.

I should drink less...Way, way less....

She thought bitterly, rubbing the yesterday's mascara off her face.

The ride wasn't too long and most was spent with her trying to clean up the mess she made by smearing her makeup all over her complexion and attempting to seek out more information from the grumpy driver. Both things went with little success and by the time she was kicked out from the Mercedes, she was as confused as she was messy.

"You look like a racoon." Were the first words that left Layton's mouth when she was escorted into the private jet by a nervous looking woman she could only guess was a flight attendant.

"Thank you very much." Sarcasm dripped off her voice like venom as she slumped down on one of billowy seats. Layton looked as flawless as ever with his thick black hair neatly groomed and stubble shaved. Even his suit looked intact, smoothened out of any wrinkles.

"I thought I told you what I think about my employees not looking the part." The words were clearly meant as a jab at her nerves. He didn't even bother to glance up from the papers he was holding.

"I thought I told you that I don't give a-"

A single glance from the cold eyed man was enough to make her swallow the remark.

"Whatever...Why the hell are we going to New York in first place!?"

"I have some business to take care of there. Didn't you read over my schedule? A very important client of mine is organizing a charity event I have to attend. A waste of money and my time, but he earns me twice as much every month..."

I can nearly feel a nasty comment forming.

"Don't make me regret bringing you instead of Angelique. She would be a prettier asset, but I was hoping for you to be tad smarter."

Ah! Here it comes.

"First of, I never asked to be dragged along to some snob event. And second, a blonde bimbo would suit you much better. Someone smart wouldn't look good by your side."

Layton's head whipped around to look her dead in the eye. If only looks could kill...

"Watch your-"

He was interrupted by flight attendant entering to offer then drinks. Catherine bumped the air with her fist in a silent victory over this argument. As childish as it was, she still had at least enough guts to tell him off.

When the stewardess left the argument was long forgotten. Or at least no longer addressed.

The glasses piled up at the small table in front of her as the flight went along. Apart from exchanging a couple of insults, the battling pair remained silent, giving her enough time to go over the events of the day before. No matter how much she tried to twist her brain, no memories came back to her, not even a flashback of going to a club.

It could be that working for Layton was traumatizing enough to drink oneself to a blackout. But there was no memories of that either.

If Nick would've been with her, he most likely would've poked fun of how she would start popping out wrinkles with how deeply she was frowning. At least she would've preferred that instead of what she got.

"Quit making that face."

"I know, I know. It'll get stuck like that."

"I couldn't care less about that. You're ruining my image."

Catherine couldn't resist rolling her eyes.

"Is there ever anyone else you think about except for you?"

"No."

"Fair enough."

Catherine followed close behind as Layton climbed down the steep stairs that lead out of the private jet. A part of her was thankful to finally get off that rattling thing, but another part was concerned with an entirely different matter that nearly begged her to go back.

I need to pee.

Those five big glasses of Pepsi did their task now it felt like her bladder would burst any moment.

"Quit dragging your feet." Layton ordered from three steps ahead, not even turning to glance at her.

"Quit bossing me around. If I'll move any faster, I'll burst."

The retort had been enough for him to finally look back at the hunched figure of his assistant.

"What do you mean burst?" He demanded for her to answer, looking as serious and annoyed as ever. It was as if he never smiled aside from when he had the chance to mock someone into obedience.

"None of your business. Just ignore me like you did."

"Tell me."

"No."

"Yes."

"No!"

"I am your supervisor. If something will prevent you from doing your job, it's your duty to tell me."

"Oh for God's sake....I need to pee!"

Many heads turned to stare at them at the announcement. Catherine felt her cheeks going red from shame.

So embarrassing!

"You'll have to hold." Layton merely shrugged, seemingly unbothered.

"No shit Sherlock."

How can one man be so damn infuriating!?

The way from the plane to the car parked nearby dragged on to the point where it seemed that they had been walking for miles. Or perhaps it was just her imagination playing tricks on her as pretty much the only thing she could think about besides her boss being a pain in the ass was the nearest bathroom.

Catherine dived into the leather seat of the black Audi, crossing her legs in a silent prayer that they'll reach the hotel or whatever place they were going to fast.

Little did she know of the adventure waiting for her ahead.

Chapter 11

"What the fuck do you mean, there's only one room left!?" Layton snarled at the shaking woman sitting at the front desk.

"I-I'm terribly sorry Mr. Grim. We're packed."

"I don't care what's your pitiful excuse. Seeing as you know my name, you sure as hell know who I am. Tell my brother to take care of this situation!"

The woman's fingers shook as she typed something away on the keyboard. Catherine could see her eyes begun to fill up with tears. Layton wasn't exactly easy to deal with. The smile she had greeted them with was long gone now, replaced by a trembling lip.

Most people gathering at the lobby had their attention turned to the front desk. They whispered among themselves or remained in wary silence.

Catherine stood leaning against one of podest used as presentators for gorgeous bush of flowers. Her defensive stance earned her quite a few critical glances from elder generation. Or perhaps it was the odd mix of pencil skirt and muddy sneakers that got their attention.

She felt like an ugly smear on a silken scarf - completely out of place. The five star hotel located at the heart of downtown Manhattan was alone enough to leave one breathless with its luxury and moneyed people casually strolling through it's halls.

In five minutes they were there, she already managed to count at least five Gucci bags.

"I'm afraid he'll be returning only in the evening...My deepest apologies, Mr. Grim. I-i'm afraid there's nothing I can do." The stutter in the counter ladies voice was answered by a long, dissatisfied sigh.

"Fine. But don't think this is over. When my brother is back, he'll hear about this. That I can promise you." Layton huffed, turning on his heel the second key made it into his hand.

Many hungry eyes of groupies followed the tall figure as he strode through the lobby. A frown suited him and that was pretty much everything Catherine had seen aside from the arrogant smirk that appeared once in thousand years when he felt victorious about something.

"Let's go." He barked an order, already jabbing the elevator button.

Catherine could only roll her eyes at the outburst. "And you call me childish. Your tantrums are no better than mine." She stole a glance backwards at the employee he had yelled at before. The brunette had been replaced and brought away to the staff room by a man in a suit who appeared to be trying to calm her down.

"It's not her fault that the rooms are taken you know."

"She screwed up the reservation. Now we're stuck in the same suite." Layton adjusted his coat, eyes fixed ahead at all times, following the movement of elevator as it closed to their floor.

Okay, maybe now I get why she should be fired.

"If you can't stand me that much, why not just free yourself of this torture that is my presence?"

"I'm not firing you. If I am, then you're going to the jail."

Well, it was worth giving a shot...

The ding of elevator arriving cut the conversation short. The pair got inside, keeping a safe distance from one another. From stranger's point of view that might even seem funny.

The elevator door begun to close, when a slender pale hand appeared in a narrow gap. The metallic door parted to reveal a head of platinum blonde hair and big brown eyes that were rimmed by black eyeliner.

From the first glance alone it was clear that she was one of these women. Seduction was what they did best and the small curve of her jungle red lips and sway in her hips as she walked inside the cramped space made it all too obvious. Her dress just barely rode her long slender legs and her cleavage nearly shouted to be noticed.

And it was.

Catherine shifted uncomfortably when Layton's eyes traveled up and down the woman's body. Not many people were above cheap sex, her being one of the rare. And him being one of those who didn't mind one bit.

"Could you press 38 for me?" The woman's voice had this timbre of upper class arrogance. And even if she looked cheap, the dress she wore wasn't.

Please...please, not in front of me.

"Of course."

Fuck...

Catherine groaned quietly as Layton leaned to press the button. What surprised her though was that aside from glancing at the woman's boobs, he showed no other desire to engage in anything. Whilst the blonde was taking joga worthy positions to push out her breasts, he simply leaned back and once again fixed his steely eyes forwards.

"My name is Judy, by the way..." She once again attempted to start a conversation, stepping slightly forwards to intrude Layton's personal space.

Boy, what a mistake that was.

"You reek of perfume.This elevator is not so small. Step back."

Catherine's eyes nearly bulged out from their sockets. This she was not expecting. And judging by how the blonde's jaw nearly hit the carpeted floor, she hadn't either.

"E-excuse me?"

"You heard."

Wow. I guess he's a d*ck to everyone.

Another ding echoed through the elevator and the door opened. She didn't pay much attention to which button Layton had pressed until they stopped at the third floor.

"Your floor." Layton glanced down at the woman with cold formality.

"B-but I said 38."

"Did you bleach your brain? Get out."

Buuurn...I feel like I time traveled to Arctics somehow.

"You rude bastard! You'll regret it!" Judy snarled, stomping out from the elevator with her high heels poking holes in the lush carpet. The door closed slowly behind her, but even then her loud cursing could be heard at least three floors up.

"Pfffftt! Hahahahaha!" Catherine doubled herself up and burst into a loud cackle of laughter. She was pretty sure it echoed through the entire hotel as the elevator took them higher to the penthouse.

Her eyes started to water and her stomach was forced to endure a series of cramps. But there was nothing she could do about it. The face the woman made, the way Layton told her off. It all was just too funny.

When she finally calmed down a little, she was fairly sure her stomach wouldn't recover for a long time. Though lack of breath wasn't the only reason. A low chuckle caught her off guard. Her blue eyes traveled up to look up at the source of her laughing fit.

A smile.

Layton Grim smiled.

The smile lingered only for a half second, just enough for her to catch a glimpse of it. Just enough for her to mistake it for an illusion, and just enough for her to realize that he had a beautiful smile.

Yet another ding interrupted her trail of thought, making her snap out from the staring contest she had unintentionally begun. The metallic door parted, revealing a sight worth millions.

Wow.

It felt like stepping into a different world. The windows encircling the large living room that would be bigger than six her apartments reached from the marble floor to ceiling, offering a breathtaking view to New York city. The thousands of lights had begun to awaken with the arrival of evening,glorifying the city in its richness.

It was a true real-estate in sky. Never in her life she had seen much more than aged apartment buildings, ran down parks and dark streets you didn't want to visit at night. This was something completely different. Out of a fairytale almost.

"Quit spacing out. If you'll keep your mouth open for any longer, you'll swallow a fly." Layton commented from somewhere behind her. At that moment nothing could ruin her mood that had gone from terrible to fantastic in matter of minutes. Or so she thought. "We're not here for fun. We're here to work. Don't forget that."

"Like you'd let me." Catherine frowned, finally turning to face Layton. He hadn't made a move to explore the suite jet. Instead he stood by the elevator with his arms crossed over his chest.

"I have some business to take care of. You'll stay here. Try not to get yourself in any trouble. And do not leave this hotel room. Did I make myself clear?"

"Yes sir!" Catherine gave a mock salute, flopping down on one of the black leather couches.

Layton didn't give out much of reaction, one last time giving her a warning look before disappearing back into the elevator. The second his cold eyes were no longer on her Cheshire smile crept onto Catherine's face.

It had been way too easy to snatch the keys from him when he was busy with Judy. And she sure as hell would use the newly gained power.

Stay put my ass. New York, here I come!

Chapter 12

The lights surrounding the city made her feel like she had traveled to a different universe. All the colors and glimmering ads created an illusion of picture perfect. Many times she had stopped to stare at the colorful tall buildings or just observed from outside how people mingled in bars and cafes, going on about their lives without a care.

Something about all that made her tad envious . She was surrounded by all this beauty and glamour, but never was meant to be part of it. She would always be just a girl from scraps, watching the world from far away.

A part of her still conflicted if what was happening would be for the good or not. Layton was without a doubt a billionaire, someone capable of either raising one's life to new heights or of destroying it completely. This time it was her balancing helplessly on the edge of the blade that could tip her over any second.

All that for a stupid cheeseburger....

Catherine sighed, rubbing her arms to get some warmth flowing into her frozen body. She had lost track of how long she had wandered about, but judging by how numb her fingers had gone, it must've been over an hour.

I can already hear all the "Where have you been!? I told you not to leave this suite!"

"Whatever...." Catherine grumbled to herself, turning on her heel to march away from the cozy cafe she had been standing outside of.

People kept pushing past her and she blended in perfectly with the grey masses, eyeing a couple bulging wallets sticking out from the pockets out of an old habit. Okay, maybe more than just that. The idea of sitting inside that cafe instead of staring at it from outside like an idiot was tempting.

Her bottom lip slowly slipped between her teeth with a deep breath. A man in his late thirties was heading right towards her, his tired gaze fixed on his cellphone. He was exhausted, with a sway in his walk, perhaps a little tipsy, having just stumbled out from a nearby bar. His coat looked nicely fitted and sewn, handmade most likely. And right in the left pocket of that coat was a familiar square outline.

There were many people around and he was the perfect target. With a soft exhale, her still fingers gripped the edge of her hood, slowly tugging it over her head. The voice in back of her head that sang not to do it was silenced completely by her slightly raising heartbeat.

The heat rose to her cheeks with every step she closed in on the man, fingers curling and uncurling inside her pocket.

One....two....BAM!

"Watch where you're going, bitch!" The man who had just passed by her snarled, not even glancing down at Catherine who now was on her fours onto the ground.

He was gone the next second and her target as well.

"Fucking bastard...." Catherine felt her blood begin to boil, hands balling into fists. It was such a good chance, ruined by some random dudes elbow!

Just my luck...

Her frown deepened at the sight of slightly bruised palms. At least she managed to break the fall before ending up face planting into a puddle. There goes the dream of warm coffee....

"Did you hurt yourself, my dear?"

Catherine's head snapped upwards towards a deep, velvety man's voice. Pale caledon eyes stared back at her from above. There was something in them that made her stomach turn in an odd way, hardly unpleasant. Rather opposite even.

"That was quite a fall. No one should be pushing a woman as beautiful as you to the ground like that."

Her attention then shifted to the nicely curved lips, man's sharp jawline and down his neck where the collar of his coat begun. Dirty blonde hair that were styled rather messily sat on head, nicely groomed stubble covering his face. There was just something about the appearance of the man and the look he gave her that left her dumbfounded.

I swear I've never gotten this horny this fast!

Catherine quickly shook her head, managing an awkward humph.

"Yeah, I'm fine." The sound of her suddenly lowering voice made her cheeks go up in flames.

I swear! What the heck is wrong with me! Sure he's hot.... very hot....Shit! Snap out of it!

"I'm glad to hear that, here, let me help you up." The smile made her heart melt on the spot. At this point she had completely forgotten that she was still on the same level as his expensive Armani dress shoes.

Tingles traveled up her arm the second the handsome stranger took a hold of her hand. His touch was gentle and warm as he pulled her up with a swift move.

"Your hands are so cold...poor thing, you're freezing to death." Instead of releasing her hand, he gently cradled it, slender fingers rubbing the cold skin of the back of her palm. Even that send odd tingles down her entire body. All thoughts of pulling away were numbed by his gentle touch.

Something about the man reminded her of Layton, but in the same time his touch was very different, gentler and there was an intent in his eyes she couldn't really read into in the moment of daze.

"If you'd like, I'd love to offer you a hot cup of coffee. My car is parked short distance away. I swear I'm not a murderer, you can trust me...."

There goes the saying "Children, don't get into stranger's car for the candy."

"You can refuse, of course...." He carried on, lifting her cold hand to his lips to blow a warm breath across the frozen skin.

Fucking hell! Do strangers usually do that!?

"I....umm....sure?"

Now, what the hell am I doing!?

Before she could bet an eye, her mouth had done the job for her and agreed to the man's offer with little to no hesitance.

For all she knew he could be a rapist or who knows what else, but the smile he gave her couldn't be resisted.

"Alright then. I couldn't have chosen better myself." The man finally released her hand, never loosing an eye contact or dropping the heart-melting smile. He moved swiftly by her side, his hand coming to rest on the small of her back.

"My name is Lucas Pierce, by the way. May I know your name?"

For a second the loud mouthed woman was of lose of words. Her brain kept spinning back to the man's hand just above her rear and the sparks that had exploded the second he touched her.

"Uhh. Catherine."

"That's a pretty name. It suites you."

I swear, this guy!

"Is it normal for you to speak in only-compliments, language?" She couldn't be sure if that was pleasant or creepy at the situation. But it most certainly worked.

Lucas chuckled, the silent laugh vibrating through his throat with deep baritone. At this she felt her knees quiver.

"Maybe." The man smirked, his pale greens coming to rest on Catherine's blue eyes. They hooked her instantly, almost making her bump into a lamp post. If it wasn't for Lucas's quick reaction, it would be the second time she would end up on the ground that day. Only this time with a bump in her head.

"But I really ever say only what I mean. It is no lie that you're beautiful."

Gulp

"Please get in." His hand suddenly left her lower back, leaving the young woman with a sinking feeling of slight disappointment. Instead, It pointed at a dark grey car parked at a sidewalk. Now, usually the idiot who did that would get a ticket in seconds, but no one dared to come near this car. It screamed 'rich' from miles away.

Where have I seen this scene before?

Layton's black car flashed through her mind, alarms going off one after another. Maybe this wasn't the best decision-

"My lady." Lucas opened the passenger door, flashing her one of those irresistible smiles.

Nah, screw it. You live only once.

Chapter 13

"So. What such a lovely creature as yourself was doing alone on New York streets?"

Catherine's head turned from the passing scenery back the the man at the wheel. Lucas's eyes were fixed on the road ahead, but she could feel him stealing glances at her with every red light.

"Dunno. Just talking a walk." She shrugged, barely forcing herself to act casual around the mysterious man. The odd tension never let up and every time his gaze landed on her she couldn't help the surge of need washing over her.

"It's not safe to wander around like that. There are many dangerous people walking those streets." There was something dark in the way he said those words, menacing even. "Good thing you stumbled upon me."

"For all I know you could be a murderer."

"I suppose so." Lucas laughed, his smirk always present. "But worry not. I wouldn't gain anything from killing such a fair lady."

Wow. He really does sort of remind me of Layton.

"You better stick to that." Catherine rejoined, her fingers never stopping their nervous play with the hem of her sleeve.

Mainly because she was afraid to touch anything else in the expensive ass car. It would be rather obvious even to a blind man that the owner had put hell of a lot work and money into the thing. The scent of leather hinted that it was brand new. She already had one billionaire to deal with. Having another one on her tail because she messed something up in his car would be too much even for her.

"We're here." Lucas announced, bringing the BMW to a halt with a mighty roar of the engine.

Catherine had been too busy studying the red and black patterns on the front panel that she had completely forgotten to keep an eye on her surroundings.

"You have got to be fucking kidding me." The words tumbled over her lips in a not-so-quiet utter when she saw the all too familiar Grand hotel.

"Is something the matter?" Lucas questioned, his perfectly shaped eyebrow raising in questioning manner.

"Yes. That is, no!" She fumbled with her words clumsily, cheeks heating up. "It's just that I happen to stay here." The nervous woman added, waving her hands to dismiss the topic. "It's just a business trip with my annoying boss. Nothing more."

Why the hell did I even say that!?

"Oh." Lucas's expression changed slightly, his smirk widening into an all out grin. "I see. Then it works perfectly." He turned off the engine before getting out from the drivers seat, leaving slightly confused Catherine behind. There was just something about him that kept unsettling her. He was more similar to a Cheshire cat by second.

"Good evening, Mr. Pierce. Allow me to take your car." A man in a red uniform offered the second the couple had gotten out from the slick auto.

"Thank you, Jorge." Lucas handed the man the key with a perfunctory smile, patting his shoulder before the pale green eyes once again zeroed in on Catherine. "Shall we?"

The young woman glanced down at the offered arm, interlocking her own with his after a fleeting moment of hesitation. She could feel solid muscles underneath his coat, brushing her upper arm with every step. Standing like this, she couldn't help but note how much taller he was than her. The top of her head barely reached to his shoulder.

Lucas payed no heed to the glances upon entering the hotel. The tall, handsome bloke strode through the halls like he owned the place. Any time they would pass an employee on their way to the elevator they would nod their heads and greet him with: "Good evening, Mr. Pierce." or "It's good to see you again, Mr. Pierce."

Catherine's suspicions climbed higher than Everest, but apart from a pointless small talk, the man didn't give a single hint of what that was all about.

Rich people.

She mentally rolled her eyes. This slick-stocking crowd was all about someone kissing up their asses. Layton and Lucas were no exception.

The elevator door opened with a familiar ding. Unlike Layton, Lucas didn't bother to keep his distance. Their arms remained locked and the man seemed to have little intention of letting go.

"There's a nice lounge. Only VIPs are allowed there. No one should interrupt. Tell me if i'm wrong with assuming that you had enough of all the crowded places. I myself prefer much more intimate setting." Lucas leaned in, his hot breath fanned across Catherine's cheeks as he whispered to her.

The heat raised in her body when his lips were so close to her skin. Close enough to be felt, but not quite touching. If it had been an intentional move, it had done just the right thing to her body, if not....it still did.

The young woman shifted on the spot, trying to ease the unmistakable tingle between her legs.

"S-sure." It's true what they say. The more you try to hide something the more it becomes apparent. Her voice pretty much gave away everything she was feeling that moment and it didn't slip past the man standing close by her side.

She could nearly feel his grin grow.

"You're so cute."

The elevator door dinged open again, revealing a spectacular view. Much like Layton's suite, the lounge had a 360 degree view to the city. No matter how many times you see it, it is still amazing, much like the building itself. The lounge was set example of the hotel's style. It was wide, luxurious and well furnished. Everything was clean to the point of sterility.

"What would you like to drink? I know I promised you coffee, but perhaps you'd like something else." Lucas finally released her arm after motioning for her to sit at one of the grey couches. Catherine nearly sunk into the soft mattress, savoring the comfort that could be offered only by higher class.

"Anything you give me will be good."

Lucas seemed so relaxed in this environment like this was his second home. Rich people were used to this kind of deal, she mused. And yet it wasn't really the setting that made her nervous. While it played a part, in the end one to blame was the man who was mixing up their drinks. Catherine had a good view of his broad back now that he had dropped his coat over the arm of a near by chair.

She could only imagine how pissed Layton will be when she will return. She could already hear him roaring across the entire hotel. Catherine seethed with annoyance just with the thought.

Who gives a fuck about him. For once I might have a shot of actually enjoying this rich lifestyle.

"So, you said you were here for business, intriguing." Lucas turned, holding two glasses of gin and tonic.

"I happen to be dragged here by my boss. I'm his assistant or whatever." Catherine grumbled, taking the glass offered to her and emptying most of it in one go.

"Or whatever?" Lucas chuckle, sounding beyond amused by what he was hearing.

"Yea. Not by choice anyhow..." Catherine said, more to herself than him. "But there ain't no point in talking about that. What about you. Are you some CEO or something?"

She was quick to change the topic, not wishing to expose more information than she already had. That and she was also getting overly distracted by the handsome blonde sitting by her side.

"I suppose I am. You see, I own this hotel."

In the very last second Catherine managed to slap a hand in front of her mouth before the drink went shooting out.

"What!? No way!" She exclaimed between coughs at which Lucas only laughed. Geez, he had a charming laughter. No women could resist those dimples on the sides of his mouth. He had this alluring vibe about him that kept drawing people in. Even when they walked through the hotel she noticed a couple lustful glances sent his way.

With Layton it was different. People feared him. Avoided him. He didn't exactly have the air of being approachable.

"Yes way. But it's nothing all that impressive."

"Are you shitting me!? You own a fucking hotel! That is ball to the ground impressive."

Lucas chuckled lowly,sipping on his tonic before setting the still full glass on the coffee table. "You have a way with words, young lady," He turned to Catherine, staring deeply into her eyes."But right now, I'm more interested in you than the hotel."

Catherine froze up in the place, her eyes going wide at the look the man was giving her. She couldn't exactly pin point his true intentions, but she was fairly certain there was a flicker of desire in his gaze.

"Umm-"

The glass was taken from her hand and gently set atop the coffee table. Something in her gut gave a sharp tug when she caught a whiff of his lemony cologne. The slender fingers brushed her own, leaving electric tingles on their wake.

He's so close!

Their gaze lasted a full second, enough for each to take in the face of the other. Nothing needed to be said, millions of years of evolution had already taken care of the message. Her lungs expended in her chest with a slow inhale. She couldn't tear her eyes off of the man now leaning over her like he had forgotten to move back when setting down the glass.

Alcohol and lust kicked in fast for the fiery soul and in short moment of notice she was already laying on her back flush against the couch with Lucas's arms on either side of her head.

"You're beautiful little toy aren't you."

Catherine found herself unable to move as if her body had been pressed down by an unknown power. She could only stare up at Lucas and watch blankly as his eyes slowly changed. She could've sworn there was a tint of red there, staining his pale green iris for a hurried second. A trick of light perhaps, but it still left her frozen in place underneath him.

"He picked good...I admit." Lucas's friendly voice had changed to something that sent shivers down her spine. If she desired to speak, she couldn't. If she wanted to move, she wasn't able to either.

Catherine's breathing picked up. She was enchanted by the man. His touch lit fire across her skin as his wide hand slipped underneath her shirt. Crawling higher, his fingertips caressed her rib cage and edge of her breast underneath the bra. All thoughts of resistance crumbled. Catherine's eyelids slowly closed as Lucas's lowered himself, his smirking lips closing in on her own until she could feel his hot breath on her.

Their faces were inches apart. She could already feel the intoxicating kiss, imagine their tongues dancing for dominance. It was so close...so...

BAM!

The door to the lounge swung open, slamming into the wall with enough force to leave a hole. The bang was like a gun shot, instantly snapping Catherine out from whatever she had fallen into. Her head snapped to the side, eyes now wide for an entirely different reason than the man towering over her.

In the door way stood a familiar broad figure of Layton Grim.

And boy, let me tell you. He did not look happy.

Chapter 14

O h...shit...

His eyes were narrowed, rigid and cold, his chest heaving with harsh breaths. Layton stood in the doorway, looking like a bull that had just seen a red rag.

Catherine could feel her face turning white as chalk, her brain stuttering the grasp the situation and potential lake of shit she had gotten herself into. His name bounced around in her skull, never making past her lips, her body yet to catch up.

She was still laying underneath Lucas, his hand still under her shirt. Only the expertise movement of his fingers had stopped. Their lips were no longer second from touching, his attention now fixed to the door as well.

"What the fuck is going on here?" Layton growled through grit teeth, pure anger seeping out from his every pore. Catherine had seen him pissed before, but not to this degree. He looked ready to break Lucas's nose.

"Well hello there, brother."

Brother!!??

Catherine's eyes zinged from one man to other, everything starting to make sense. It should've already when Lucas mentioned being the owner of the hotel, but no, she had to fall for his spell of seduction. Acute embarrassment washed over her, all desire gone with snap of fingers.

"You did not answer my question." Layton stalked inside the lounge, his hands clenched in fists by his sides and muscles of his jaw moving with every clench of his teeth. He looked like he was ready to punch the living hell out of Lucas.

"What does it look like? You have never been good at taking care of your toys, I figured I would do it fr you. I found this one wandering around on streets." Lucas withdrew his hand from underneath her shirt, sitting up with a casual shrug of his shoulders.

Layton's hawk like gaze whipped towards Catherine, piercing through her like a sword. "I thought I told you not to go anywhere." He glared down at her, disregarding the following comment from Lucas.

"Aren't you overly protective." The smirking man had returned to sipping his tonic with little care, slight amusement dancing in his pale green eyes upon his brother's wrath.

"We're going." Layton grabbed Catherine's wrist, pulling her onto her feet with a sharp tug.

"Ouch! Hey! I am not your–"

"Keep your mouth shut." His growl left her stunned, giving him the moment to drag her away from the lounge before she could even manage one last glare at Lucas.

"Like hell I will! Let go of me!" Catherine struggled, digging her toes in the floor just for the man to release her, but it was all in vain. His head remained turned away from her, not a single word voiced, which was even worse than his yelling at her. He pushed her around like a rag doll, his angered expression never leaving his features.

"I am not your damn puppet! Let me go, you're hurting me!"

Finally his grip loosened after they had entered their shared suite after the terrific trip through the hotel with people staring and whispering behind their back. Layton hadn't payed any attention to that, nor the woman's intense protests.

"If you wanted to fuck someone, you could've picked any-one but him." He turned to face her, the vehemence in his eyes leaving her confused.

"I did not want to fuck anyone! And even if I did, it would be none of our damn concern!" Catherine felt her own anger boiling up. She was no pushover and yet that was how she was treated as. As a 'toy'.

"I am not your toy or anyone's! What the hell was even that for!? You think because you're rich and I stole your wallet you have some sort of saying over me!? You must be nuts, man." Catherine returned Layton's glare, keeping her stance straight as she observed the man's expression slowly changing from one of anger to something she couldn't quite read.

"You're wrong, spitfire."

The next second she found herself being lifted off of the ground. The floor and ceiling spun before she found herself bouncing off of a soft mattress of the bed.

"You're mine." Layton was now the one towering over her with his mighty built. "I have all the power to keep you here and do as I wish."

"You fucking pervert, get off of me-"

Layton's hands reached out, pinning her wrists to the mattress when she tried to push him off of her. He was a great deal stronger and no amount of struggling could get her to escape this situation. She was trapped underneath his bulk.

His eyes had turned dark, clouded by something she feared to see. This man was dangerous and she had crossed his limits of patience. Now, she was ought to regret it.

"You're mine." He repeated, his grip tightening to the point of being bone crashing.

Catherine's whimper was silenced by lips suddenly pressing up against her own. The kiss was demanding and rough, leaving her breathless. His tongue broke past her lips,intruding into her mouth to caress her own. Her eyes widened and muscles tensed.

She had been in this situation before. She knew where it lead, how crippling the result was.Catherine felt the panic begin like a cluster of spark plugs in her abdomen. Tension grew in her face and limbs, her mind replaying the last attack. Her eyes begun to water with the sudden violation.

She had escaped once and promised herself to never end up in this situation again. Her body acted on his own, her head turning to the side and teeth catching Layton's bottom lip.

Metallic blood seeped into her mouth before the man was pulling away as sharply as he had came at her. Layton now stared directly into her wide eyes again, his lip split from her bite and eyes wild. There was a familiar heat in them that disappeared on an instant upon seeing her expression.

Long moment of silence followed with neither moving a muscle before he finally stood back up. His back was once again turned to her, shoulders raising and falling with each breath.

"Go to sleep. We have a lot of work to do tomorrow."

It was all he said. It was all he had to say. The door banged shut behind him, leaving Catherine alone in the dark bedroom. She stared up at the ceiling, still tasting fresh blood on her lips. Her form was shaky, panic attack threatening to surge up again.

There no way she would be falling asleep that night.

Chapter 15

The sharp blues rested calmly on all too familiar laptop screen, skimming over a report to witch finding a meaning would be like discovering protein in lettuce. A long sigh slipped past the man's lips, his hand raising to pinch between his eyes. He had hired best of the best and a couple pointless sentences was all they could give him.

Dark circles sat underneath his eyes, signs of exhaustion unmistakable. It had been a long night of him sleeping on a couch. And the sleeping part was in fact him attempting to do some more office work. Boring enough to exhaust, yet demanding for certain concentration.

He couldn't get the previous day's events out from his head. It was nothing out of ordinary for him to easily go from zero to hundred, but even for Layton, his reaction had been too harsh. Messing with his new assistant had become one of his ways of entertainment in otherwise boring-to-tears existence. She was easy to tease and reacted rather badly to his every comment. The woman was childish which made it all that more unbelievable that he had become so possessive of her.

Idly, his eyes raised to look at the usually bubbly woman sitting across from him in the car. It was hard to shut her up, but now she hadn't said a single word or even looked at him. Her eyes were distant, gazing at the passing buildings. She wasn't even his type. And yet he found her oddly intriguing. Even he couldn't deny her looks.

Layton's eyes did a quick scan. The lady suit he had picked for her accented her body rather well. He almost let a grin slip onto his features when his stare landed on her feet. The high heels were kicked aside. She really hated wearing those.

"What are you staring at?" Her voice came to life, Layton's gaze switching upwards to meeting with an all too familiar glare. The look was far different from the one she had given to him last night. No woman had ever looked so terrified when approached by him. They melted under his touch, but she had resisted like her life depended on it.

"Making sure you haven't lost your shoes. They are-"

"Expensive." Catherine finished his sentence, rolling her eyes. "I learned from the first time." She grumbled, turning back to the window.

"Don't get me wrong. I have no interest in someone like you." Layton switched back to his laptop, frown now plastered on his face.

"Is that why you harassed me last night?"

"You have to know not to get involved with people you shouldn't even talk to. My siblings specially." Layton's voice was of ice, long fingers already working their way across the keyboard.

"'I am Mr. Arrogant's brother' wasn't written on his forehead when I met him." Catherine growled back, earning herself a quick glare.

"Nothing like that would've happened if you obeyed and stayed at the suite. Didn't your parents teach you not to go with strangers?"

"I have no parents."

Pause.

Layton's eyes momentary shifted back to the young spitfire. Both of them fell silent again, Catherine doing her best to look anywhere but at the man sitting across from her.

"I'm just telling you to be careful." His voice had a low rumble to it, his nature doing little to break the ice between them.

"Are you worried?" He couldn't read Catherine's voice, but he was certain she was to taunt him about this in couple of seconds. Something he couldn't allow.

"I can't let you ruin my image." There was a dismissive shrug of his shoulders, eyes fixed back on the screen. Layton did not react any to Catherine's scoff as the car was brought to a halt in front of the all too familiar hotel.

The morning had been busy with meetings and now he had to attend one he was looking forwards to the least.

"Go to the suite. There's a dress prepared for you for the evening gala."

"You're buying me dresses now?"

"You'll be my escort. I can't allow you to look bad. Don't think you're special."

The limo door opened, hotel staff meeting them with a polite greeting. Catherine shook her head, looking fed up with everything as she got out of the car with shoes in one hand. She stormed ahead, grumbling underneath her breath as Layton watched.

"Mr. Grim," One of the staff approached, just barely having the gut to keep an eye contact. "Mr. Pierce is expecting you."

"I'm aware." At his clipped response the employee only gave a silent nod, stepping back to give way to the sharply dressed business man. Layton wore black suits like others wore t-shirts. Little effort needed to be put into him pulling out the look of successful billionaire he was.

Lucas was much more lied-back. More of a type to sport leather jacket rather than business attire. And that was exactly what Layton found his brother wearing upon entering the lounge.

Phone in hand and feet propped up on coffee table, Lucas Pierce lounged across the very couch which had caused so many events to take place the day before. He didn't even glance up from the expensive device when Layton spoke.

"Let's make this as short as possible. What did you want?" Obvious irritation could be heard in his voice. He was not the type to be summoned like a loyal dog. His brother requesting a meeting was just another headache.

"Is that how you greet family? Oh come on, be a little sweeter at once." Lucas grinned, pale eyes sparking with tease that was returned by a sharp glare from the other man.

"Alright, alright. Just wanted to set everything up for the action. There are some nice souls coming in this year. Quite a few to even suit your taste."

"Couldn't you text me the details? I don't have to meet you in person for this." The dissatisfaction grew by second, reflecting in his words and voice.

"Geez, you're cold. Poor Catherine. I can only imagine ow it is to work for you." Lucas set down his phone, smile still sticking to his lips, tempting Layton to wipe it right off.

"It's none of your business how I treat my employees. I suggest you stay away from her."

"Jealous much? Don't worry, I have enough toys of my own. I was just curious." Lucas took a glass of what Layton assumed was whiskey and took a sip. "She's a cute girl. Not really your type though."

"What do you think you know about who's my type." Layton growled, feeling his anger boiling up.

"So you do like her."

"This conversation is over. Mail me the details about the action, and don't bother me to satisfy your damn curiosity." He turned towards the door, only to be stopped in tracks by Lucas's next words.

"You should be careful. Vatican is on your tail. She's your weakness."

Layton glanced back to see two piercing greens staring back, smile now gone from his brother's face.

"I'll be the judge of that."

Chapter 16

T his is stupid. Why should I attend some random gala?

"Please don't frown. I can't put on your make up." The woman who had been working on Catherine's face for the past hour grumbled, patience just barely holding by the thread after having heard all the complaints. The woman was an exceptionally difficult client and wouldn't shut up for a god damn second.

"This is dumb. I feel like I have a cake on my face."

"Miss, please don't move."

"I ain't moving! You're the one poking my eye out!"

"Ugh. That's it. I'm done." The makeup artist announced, glaring daggers at the woman in the chair.

"Oh, thank God!" Catherine sighed. The seething from the other woman fell on deaf ears as she sprung up from the uncomfortable chair. Layton had ordered a makeup artist and a hairdresser to attend to her looks. Quote: 'To make her presentable'.

If it hadn't been for his comment of how she looked like a raccoon that's been it by a truck, perhaps she wouldn't be that mad.

That fucking bastard!

Catherine fumed, her gaze meeting the mirror for the first time. The reflection had her jaw dropping. She could hardly recognize herself. Dare she say, she looked like one of those models on VOGUE.Her unruly brunette hair were arranged in a neat bun, strands of loose hair sitting on either side of her painted face. Her sea blue eyes were rimmed by dark eyeliner that made them pop.

For a second she was stunned, all racing thoughts of how she hated Layton coming to a halt. Perhaps this was not so bad.....

No. It is bad. Only I look good.

An obviously overpriced gown lied atop the bed, waiting to complete the glamorous look. Dress of silky black.

"That must cost a fortune....." Catherine murmured, fingers running across the cool, soft material.

"It does."

"Wha-" Catherine swiveled around at the deep voice coming from behind her.

"Jeez, you nearly gave me a heart attack. Don't you know it's not good to sneak up on people?" She grumbled, glaring at the dark haired man. Layton simply scoffed.

"Get dressed. We have to go soon."

Her eyebrow arched upwards. She had gotten used to his dominating ways, but nothing could change how annoying it was. "And you're going to watch?" Catherine crossed her arms, trying to keep on the best glare she could master.

"I could." Layton's expression hardly changed. Still cold and stoic. But the devious look in his eyes had her stepping back to grab onto the nearest hard object she could fling across the room.

"I dare you to try."

"Put down the lamp." Layton sighed, already turning to return to the living room. "And hurry up. We don't have time for this."

The door shut behind him, the footsteps growing more distant as the man retreated to the other room. She could never read him. He could go from ice cold to fire hot in a second. He was beyond annoying! And arrogant! God, somebody had inflated his ego like a balloon and she couldn't find a needle to pop it.

But he's handsome too....Tall, muscular...No. Stop. He's a fucking devil!

Catherine shook her head, returning to stare at the dress. When she got dressed, she had lost all sights of the girl in torn leather jacket and dirty sneakers. She was elegant, her slender frame kissed by the silk of the dress. The fabric swirled around her legs with every step, the slit to the side teasing with an occasional show of her legs.

She could hardly picture what Nick would say of he saw her like this. For him, she was like a rebellious little sister. He had never seen her looking anything like a lady, which made her wish he would be here, just so she could take a picture of his face and frame it.

"Why do women always have to wear killers of shoes? They're already a pain in a butt-" Catherine grumbled as she exited the bathroom. Layton was standing in front of another mirror in the living room, fixing his dark grey tie. His short black hair were slicked back. The clenched jaw made the high cheekbones appear highlighted, the sharp features manly and clean shaved. The five o'clock shadow he sported in the morning was gone, leaving behind smooth skin. He emitted raw power and everything about his screamed - billionaire.

"Maybe they wouldn't be if you didn't put them in your butt." Layton retorted, his icy gaze meeting hers through the reflection in mirror. The movement on his expertise fingers paused as he stared.

Catherine shifted uncomfortably. He was staring. Layton didn't even bother to be subtle about how his eyes scanned her like an x-ray.

The man was freaky, but thank God he couldn't see trough her dress. For some reason his eyes alone set her skin on fire. The events of previous night came rushing back. The make up didn't allow the flush on her cheeks show as she remembered how his muscular bulk towered over her frame. It had been intimidating, scary....and something else she was not going to name.

"You look good." Layton's baritone rung through the suite, the words making her blink in near disbelief.

"Was that a compliment?"

"Don't get cocky. You look good enough to stand by my side, that's all." He huffed arrogantly, tugging on his suit to straighten it of none existent wrinkles.

"Oh, too late. I heard it. Don't try to cover it up. You think I'm pretty." Catherine grinned,haughty.

Layton simply dismissed her by a roll of his eyes and a low grumble which she couldn't really make out. "Let's go. This is an important event and I can't afford to be late." He stretched out his arm, signalling her to take it.

"What are we holding hands now?"

"Shut up and take it. You're my escort for the night. You have to be by my side a all times. I can't trust someone as clumsy to wander around on their own." Layton smirked at the angry twitch of her eyebrow.

"I'm not clumsy." Catherine murmured, her hand easily slipping into his. Strange. Her smaller hand fit so nicely in his larger one. His grip on her was surprisingly gentle as well as he guided her arm to entwine with his.

What's up with him? He is never this gentle. What is he plotting?

Catherine glanced at him suspiciously as they walked out from the suite. She was in heels that could stab someone and yet he still towered over her by a good head and shoulders. His cologne wafted over her. He smelled fresh and masculine, slightly minty as well.

"You're staring." Layton noted as they got into the elevator.

"No I'm not." Catherine quickly averted her gaze, something else catching her interest. His lips. The night before she sunk her teeth into his bottom lip. She clearly remembered the taste of his blood on her tongue. And yet there wasn't a single mark there.

"Yes you are." Layton turned to her. "If you want a kiss, you will have to work harder for it."

"W-what. Who said I want to kiss you. You're the pervert out of the two of us." Catherine hissed, glaring at him through the long, fake lashes the make up artist had stuck to her eyelids.

"You angered me."

"And that gives you the right to harass me-" Her rant was cut short by a 'ding' of door opening. Layton had turned his attention away from her, no longer listening to her complaints. His expression had gone back to normal as he lead the way. Catherine seethed quietly, still pissed by now busy concentrating on not tripping over the edge of her dress and topple down like a fool.

Expecting him to apologize was like waiting for a pumpkin to turn into a twenty dollar bill.

"Mr. Grim." A man in a black suit greeted Layton as they approached large two sided door. Music could be heard leaking through the cracks with the chatter of many people. Catherine felt nervousness building as the man opened the door for them, revealing a sight that left her stunned.

Wow...

Ginormous, glittering hall stretched ahead of her, bustling with equally glamorous people. Nervousness had turned her into a barely moving stick already and they hadn't even stepped inside the party hall.

Boy, oh, boy....this is going to be a fucking looong night.

Chapter 17

"Relax. You're so stiff that I could've chosen a broom for my escort instead of you." Layton's deep voice sounded in her ear, a low warning whisper.

"Easy for you to say. And I never asked to be here in the first place. You could've taken that broom." Catherine protested, her eyes wide as five cent coins. The hall hosted dozens upon dozens of guests. She could barely take a step not to trip over someone. Colors of expensive gowns made her feel like she had an unicorn for dinner and now she was high.

This was scary. The setting was enough to give one a social anxiety.

"We are not discussing this now. There are many important figures here tonight. Mind your manners." Layton growled, his hand moving from holding her own to the low of her back. Their sides pressed together as he lead her through the crowd. She was too nervous to object, seeking at least some comfort from his warmth.

The air was thick. Many curious eyes were drilling holes into the pair, some guests not bothering to mask their brewing gossip. On their way to the table, they were approached by countless of overly rich people. All of them treated Layton as if he was a God, giving him their greetings and attempting to arrange a meeting, which he disregarded with a simple glare.

"Mr. Grim. My wife and I would be happy to welcome you and your pretty partner in our humble home." A man Layton had just bumped into spoke. He looked like a Barbies boyfriend, only fifty years older and with butt implants. Someone who could afford such monstrosity on themselves certainly had a lot of access cash. Maybe that's why Layton let the man speak.

Catherine could feel his fingers dig into her side, jaw clenching in mild annoyance. The old man didn't even notice the deadly look Layton was sending his way.

"I am certain we could-"

"I am certain we won't." Layton finally snapped, now looking pissed. "Quit wasting my time, Mr. Bart. We have had this conversation and I am not interested." Layton simply stepped to the side, dragging Catherine with him as he stomped off.

And I should mind my manners....

"Burn...." Catherine whispered silently, slightly amused. "I thought there were many important snobs here and we should mind what we say." She teased, the grin on her face contrasting on the scowl Layton was sporting.

"He was not worth my time." The man said simply, releasing her waist. Finally they had reached their table. It was positioned in front of a small podium with a speaker on it and a couple of people were already sitting there, one of which she recognized instantly.

"Ah, finally you two came." Lucas smiled widely, oozing fake innocence. "Took you long enough." His voice was a teasing purr as he sat with his arms propped on the armrests. He wore a silvery grey suit with striking red tie. The blonde hair were styled messily, but kept neat and combed. Just like the first time she saw him, he looked gorgeous.

At his side sat a beautiful woman with long red hair and deep brown eyes. She was messing with her nails until she saw Layton and turned her attention to eye-raping the other brother.

"Shut up." Layton growled, taking his seat without another glance at his brother. If it was even possible, he looked even more grumpy than he did before.

"That's my sunshine of a brother." Lucas grinned, sarcasm dripping off his alluringly low voice.

Catherine was left standing, confused, watching the exchange awkwardly before Lucas's pale green orbs landed on her.

"Catherine! You look gorgeous. I thought you looked beautiful when I saw you, but now I am lost for words. Take a seat."

His intense gaze made the woman shift uncomfortably. There was just something about the man that made her wary. "Right...." She murmured, a bit clumsily landing in a seat besides irritated looking Layton. "Lost for words...clearly." He grumbled, giving Lucas a pointed look.

They were brothers but their relationship was closer to a disaster than anything else.

The atmosphere quickly grow tense. With the shameless flirting of Lucas and Layton's constant jabs, Catherine turned her attention to the mingling crowd instead of the two handsome men acting like five year old boys.

Everyone was starting to take their places at the tables, exchanging pointless conversations.

This is boring. Catherine noted, her gaze suddenly stopping at a strange figure lurking around the more shadowy part of the hall. She frowned. A man dressed all in black was staring intensely at their table, his motionless eyes meeting hers.

The woman felt her skin crawl. There was something terribly eerie about the man. Eyes of palest watery blue, like a creature who's spent it's life in perpetual shadow, the stranger was gazing at her without blinking once. His figure was shrouded by passing people, seemingly unable to notice his presents, and shadows of decorative pillars.

Her eyebrows furrowed, all conversations held only a blur to her ears. There was something that didn't allow her to avert her gaze as the man lifted a single unnaturally long, thin finger to his chapped lips. He mouthed something. Sitting too far away, she couldn't make out his words, but they gave her the type of creeps you get from horror films.

"Cavenon." A light tap on her knee made her whip around, to find Layton glaring at her. "Sit straight, It's starting."

Catherine sighed, turning back to the table, but not before taking another glance at the man. He was no longer standing there. Gone like a mirage in desert.

Creepy....

The woman turned her attention back to front. The lights in the hall dimmed as an elderly man stepped onto the podium to address the guests. She didn't really listen to what he was saying, her thoughts occupied with what she had just witnessed.

One speech went by after another when the final speaker finally announced that the dinner is about to be served. The woman had zoomed out most of the time, her thoughts elsewhere, at least until now. Finally, something to be excited about. Catherine's face lit up. Food for free! Maybe this party wasn't so bad after all!

Wrong.

When the waiter placed a plate down in front of her, she was horrified.

"They serve snails?!" She exclaimed, turned to Layton who barely showed any emotion at the served meal.

"They are specially ordered and are very expensive. You should try them. Looks worse than it is." Lucas explained calmly, having heard the horror in her voice. The red head at his side was chuckling, giving Catherine a mean look. "Is this your first time trying out a delicacy, poor thing."

"You call snails a delicacy. I would be more concerned about you." Catherine glared at the amused woman, refusing to be bullied by some rich skunk.

"Don't talk so loud." Layton pinched her knee, making her flinch.

"Will you stop doing that?!"

"I will when you keep your lips zipped." Layton growled, pinching her again. He might look irritated, but she saw the teasing glimmer in his eyes. He was enjoying messing with her. Catherine frowned. Two could play this game.

Her hand reached out, about to pinch Layton's leg when a strong hand caught her by the wrist. His steely eyes bore into her with obvious warning. "Don't make me regret bringing you along, spitfire."

"You two are adorable." Lucas commented, cutting short the stare contest the two had begun. Layton ignored him, dismissing his brother with a scoff. His hand released hers, leaving behind white fading marks. Catherine rubbed her wrist, the snails on her plate once again having the full attention.

The number of cutlery set besides her plate got her head spinning. Why couldn't they just give her a single fork instead of five!?

Catherine stole a side glance at Layton. He wasn't eating, instead his gaze was fixed elsewhere. Sighing, she picked a random fork. Might as well taste the 'delicacy'. Her face twisted in disgust as she tried to stab one of the snails. They were still inside their shell, making it near impossible mission.

After chasing a slippery snail through the plate for near five minutes, she felt her blood begin to boil. Angry, she sent the fork down with full force. It hit the plate, causing the snail to fly off.

All she could do was to watch it plop into the red heads wine glass. The woman had been busy chatting with Lucas and hadn't noticed until the glass rose to her jungle red lips. Catherine felt the cringe creeping in on her as she took the sip, frowning at the sudden strange taste.

"What's up with this wine? It tastes odd. A new brand?"

Oh shit!

Catherine's shoulders hunched, teeth biting down on her tongue. The shake in her shoulders gave it away - she barely resisted tipping her head back and roaring in laughter.

She felt her cheeks heating up. This was just too funny!

"Ha!" Catherine slapped a hand in front of her mouth, a second too late. The laugh had already slipped, causing everyone at the table to look at her like she had a couple screws missing. Well, everyone, but Layton who had witnessed her show. His expression couldn't be read. It remained stone like aside from a slight tilt of his lip. Was he...amused?

Even if he was, the emotion was gone as soon as it appeared, the strictness returning. "You're unbelievable." He grumbled, taking a sip of his own drink. "Hopefully you didn't get a snail into my glass as well."

"My aim was slightly off." Catherine spoke through heavy breaths, her eyes wet with tears at their wake. God, this party was better than she had anticipated it to be.

"That woman is strange..." The red head murmured to Lucas, who also looked a tad amused, having caught glimpse of the flying snail. That woman was something else.

"Excuse me." Another voice chimed in behind Catherine.

A middle aged man had approached them, looking over the group with calm, grey eyes. He was one of the guests. The tailored suit fit his lean frame and his hair peppered with grey were combed back in an elegant way. The man was leaning against a wooden cane with wolfs head engraved on the top.

He looked like one of those wise men in movies that turned out to be evil in the end. His eyes lingered on the woman sitting besides Layton, before the grey orbs trailed to the man himself. "Mr. Grim, I was hoping you would come." The man smiled.

Somehow he left her with an uneasy feeling in the pit of her stomach.

"Of course." Layton spoke, getting up from his seat, for her great surprise. The man was the first guest he actually payed attention to.

"Good that I find you so early on. We could discuss business and then I shall leave you to enjoy the party." The man suggested, his stiff smile never wavering.

From time to time his eyes traveled to Catherine as he waited for the man's answer. Layton nodded, briefly turning to face his escort.

"I will come back. Stay put and don't talk to anyone."

"Wai-"

And with that he left along with the strange man, not even caring to hear what she had to say.

Cool....now I'm alone here...

The woman felt a nervous churn in her stomach. Somehow uneasiness didn't leave her alone and as far as she knew the only thing she had to be concerned about was the red head discovering the snail in her glass.

And she did.

Chapter 18

A long, tired sigh escaped her plumps lips. Delicate fingers gripped the side of marble sink she was leaning against. Catherine had managed to swiftly escape to the nearest bathroom when the red head threw a fit. It was funny until she decided to send the glass of wine flying in her direction. Thank God for Lucas who managed to grab her just on time.

She did not belong here. Being a street rat almost seemed easier than this. It was tough, but at least she knew that world. She knew what it took to survive when every day was a new struggle for basic needs. Surrounded by luxury and riches was terrifying. Even her face had been painted beyond recognition.

Layton had just left her there alone without a word. That asshole...

Catherine groaned, finally mustering enough courage to leave the bathroom. The hallway was empty. Honestly she didn't know where she had ran off to in her haste.

Again, the looming feeling of danger had her blood freezing over.

Stop it you coward....Your nerves are finally catching up, 'is all-

Suddenly the lights around her flickered, some bulbs never coming back to life. The light drained. There was barely enough even for shadows. The young woman froze on the spot. The hallway was suddenly dark and silent. It was the kind of silence that falls right before you get knifed in the back.

Thump....thump...thump....

A bead of cold sweat formed on her brow as footsteps approached from behind. Quiet, light and eerie. Perhaps the red-head had come to murder her about the snail. That would be the best option from those rushing through her head.

Slowly, she turned.

A grimy figure stood on the other end of the hallway, pale eyes pinning her down. She knew those eyes. They had stared at her with the same thirst for blood in the gala. No words were required. She knew on the instant that her life was in grave danger, even before she saw the shine of a knife in his pale hand.

Woman's body kicked into motion. Her mind ceased it's unproductive buzz, now providing her with adrenaline and calculations of how to get out from this mess. The heels were left behind with little care as the female begun to sprint down the dark hall.

The hallway curled away into infinite dark. With a killer hot on her heels, she hardly cared for the lack of light anymore or for the reason he was there in the first place. She ran for her life, stopping only to tug on random door to see if there was any way to escape back to the ball party and seek help.

"Fuck." Her lips produced a desperate curse when another door refused to budge.

Catherine took a quick look over her shoulder, nervous gaze scanning the hallway where the man had been standing. He wasn't there anymore. Was she losing her mind? Seeing things? It had been years since she last touched drugs and yet there she was, hallucinating.

"What the hell...." Her muscles relaxed for a brief moment, her mind trying to catch up on what had just happened.

The young woman took a step back from the door, still confused and shaken. She had a very solid reason to be scared.

With the first backwards step, she felt presents right behind her.

A pale hand reached out from darkness, clasping in front of her mouth. A muffled scream and rustle of her struggle could be heard down the hall as she was forced against the man's front, her back pressing against his oddly cold body.

Catherine's body twisted and turned, her every move a pure instinct as the man held her firmly. She could hear his wheezing breath in her ear, his other hand raising to her throat with a sharp knife held between his stiff fingers.

Her eyes widened. She felt the cold metal press against her neck.

Her fingers dug into his arm in a feeble attempt to pull it away. The man was strong despite his scrawny frame. The cold metal hovering inches from her neck made it near impossible to not panic. It scratched against her skin, seconds away from slicing it open.

Her body made the decision for her. She was not about to die from the hand of a silent killer. Not after everything she has been through.

Her head moved back with force, colliding painfully with the man's nose. Her hair fell loose from the bun, swirling in the air around her as she took the fleeting moment to get away from the assailants grip.

The knife nicked her throat, warm drops of ruby red beginning to leak out and run down in thin trickles.

The man behind her groaned, manufacturing the first human-like sound during their interaction. His grip loosened, allowing Catherine to evade the deathly grip.

She stumbled away, Layton's words of her being clumsy proving themselves on the worst time possible. Her foot got caught in her long dress, successfully tripping her over. The world rushed by in a blur, hurriedly approaching impact inevitable. Gravity pulled the young woman to the ground, her head slamming against the hard flooring.

Her lips parted in a silent scream. Strong, dull pain rushed through her skull like electricity. Her vision clouded over, all her limbs suddenly paralyzed. The back of her head throbbed, all senses distorted.

Through the blur she saw a movement, two black shoes coming into her line of sight. She drew in a sharp breath, single through passing through her aching head.

I am screwed....

Her eyes closed. She much rather not see what would happen.

"To think someone of your status would send such lowly creature after her....I'm disappointed." A low, familiar voice cut through the silence.

Her heart fluttered, heavy eyelids slowly peeling open to see a tall figure in distance. First time she was genuinely happy to see Layton. He stood at the end of dark hallway, the shorter man he had left with cowering behind him.

The feeling of relief was short-lived, quickly replaced by utter horror. The man who had been sent to kill her suddenly disappeared, pile of ashes sitting where his shoes once were. Catherine held her breath, fighting to stay conscious as the two men approached.

"My Lord...It's not how it looks like!" The older man ex-claimed. "I wouldn't dare! Grim family is very respected-"

"Quit flapping your gums, old man, before I cut your tongue out." Layton growled, his voice growing nearer.

Catherine shut her eyes, listening in carefully.

"P-please, My Lord. This is a misunderstanding. I wouldn't dare to send an assassin after a soul that belongs to you." The old man stuttered, sounding terrified.

A soul??

"Leave." Layton commanded, his words final.

"Y-yes, my Lord."

Catherine felt someone kneel besides her with a sigh. Familiar scent of cologne tickled her fuzzy senses.

"You're nothing but trouble, spitfire." Layton whispered, gently placing her into his arms. "I can't leave you alone for a damn minute." Her body was easily lifted up, strong arms wrapping around her protectively. "And she lost her shoes again..." Layton grumbled under his breath.

Catherine could no longer force her eyes to open. Her consciousness was slipping as he carried her. Nothing was certain anymore, but one thing - what she had seen was not a hallucination. It had been real.

Layton Grim was not human.

Chapter 19

"She's going to find out eventually...Unless you keep deleting her memories." A voice broke through the darkness, sounding quiet and distant.

"She's a human. She can't know." Another, lower, voice spoke.

"Look at you, caring for her."

"Don't be stupid."

The voices became clearer, recognizable. One clearly belonged to Layton and the other could be his brother. "Then you're just going to wipe out her memories every time someone sends an assassin? Poor thing, she's going to forget all the fun parts."

"She would be even bigger pain in the ass if she knew."

If I knew what?

Catherine frowned in her sleep, consciousness slowly overtaking the darkness.

"Look, someone's waking up." Lucas noted. She could hear the grin in his voice and already sense frown on Layton's features.

Her eyes fluttered open. She was laying on her side on the couch, her bare shoulders covered by a suit jacket. Layton sat across from her, his muscular arms crossed over the broad chest and the usual scowl plastered on his face. Lucas stood couple steps away, still fully dressed in the silvery suit he wore to gala. Only the red tie was loosened and a glass of whiskey had made it into his hand.

"Good morning sleeping beauty." Lucas was first to speak, lady killer smile coming to life on his lips. "You got us worried. That fall was impressive."

Catherine felt her head pulsating unpleasantly. Whatever they weren't telling her, at least this was the truth, she did bang her head pretty hard. "What happened..." Slowly she sat up, wincing at the sudden sharp pain on her neck. Unconsciously her fingers caressed the wound. It was already bandaged and treated.

"You disobeyed me and wandered off, hit your head and we found you unconscious." Layton cut in before Lucas could come up with his version of the story. Impressive, his face didn't even change iota when he lied.

Catherine glared at the man, carefully sitting up to face him. The jacket placed over her shoulders slid down to her side, robbing her of it's warmth. "Is that so?" Her voice leaked heavy suspicion. "I am not buying that. I remember what happened. I was almost killed!" Her glare matched Layton's, fury tinting her sea blue eyes.

The man sitting on the couch across from her sighed, pinching between his eyes. "Of course you do." He stood slowly, the towering built making Catherine feel small in comparison. She did not flinch away like most would when given a glare by Layton Grim himself. The pair had butted heads enough for her to get used to him trying to intimidate her.

"You're leaving me with no other choice." He took a step closer, making her alert. "Tomorrow we're going back to Seattle and you won't remember this evening."

Lucas sighed, watching the exchange. "Greed, this is not right."

Greed?

Catherine stood up, ignoring the slight dizziness. "No. You have to explain what is going on. Who the fuck are you?"

"It's none of your business."

"Like hell it isn't! Some creepy dude almost stabbed me and you're trying to say it's none of my business!?" This exchange got her dander up in a second. "You dragged me into this! I never asked to be your assistant, or have my memory deleted or whatever! I deserve an explanation. Now!" Her demand rung loud and clear, fire in her eyes never easing as she stared at her boss.

Silence befell the room. Both men looked at her, intensely. Lucas was like a child, watching an exciting movie, sipping casually on his drink while observing the two argue. The girl had guts.

Layton's reaction was way better masked, but the brief pause gave away his surprise at the sudden snap. Only this woman dared to talk like that to him. Even his siblings were hesitant to go against him, but not her.

"Alright." He grumbled after a pause.

Lucas nearly choked on his drink. His brother was the stubbornest man alive and yet he caved in. A near historical moment! The intensity of light haired man's exhilaration grew. There was no way he was going to miss this.

Catherine had not expected him to agree so easily either. It took every bit of control to keep a straight face and not lose her determination to brief sense of victory.

"You might want to sit down for this." Lucas commented, earning himself a pointed look from Layton.

The young woman shifted impatiently. "So then...What are you?" The nervous note in her voice couldn't be hidden easily. Her insides churned with worry and head buzzed with thousand questions.

"We are not humans. We are sins." Layton said as if was the most simple thing on Earth. His cold eyes bore into Catherine's frozen figure. The young woman was left stupefied. She could only stare at him with still eyes, daring only shallow breaths.

"W...what?"

Her gaze trailed off to the other man in the room, seeking proof that she wasn't the only one hearing this. Lucas had a more serious expression on his face as he nodded. "It's true."

Her knees buckled, forcing her to sit back down on the couch.

"Humans are too slow witted to see the real world around them. They live in blissful peace unaware of creatures like us. Until someone as clumsy as you comes along and screws it all up."

"So you're like a character from Bible or something?"

I should've gone to church when I had the chance!

Catherine rubbed her face, any thoughts of messing up her make up long gone. She looked like a panda since the beginning of the evening anyway. This was a lot to take in. She knew there was something off about them, but hadn't expected this.

Lucas chuckled at her question, finding it amusing. "Bible describes only one side of us. It's like a biography written by a distant relative you've seen once. Most of it isn't true."

"Humans are too ignorant to write about us." Layton added, making her frown. Mr. Arrogant was still living up to his name. In any other situation she would've argued, but the chaos in her head forced out the first random question it could muster instead. "What sin are you?"

"Greed."

"That explains a lot."

Lucas let out an entertained laugh, turning a blind eye to the dirty look his brother was giving him. "She's gold." He said between chuckles. "If you wouldn't be so possessive of your toys I would ask to borrow her. Not that it's worth asking anything from Greed."

"I am not his toy." Catherine protested. She already had an idea of what sin Lucas was. Their first encounter was starting to make sense now. He was Lust. The missing puzzle pieces begun to fall in place.

"What about my memories then?" Her voice dropped to a whisper. "How can you...erase them?"

"Every sin is born with a gift. I can seduce anyone regardless of age or gender and make them do what I desire. Layton can manipulate memories, make people forget who they are." Lucas explained calmly, proud of his gift.

That jerk used it on me! Unbelievable!

Catherine paused before any insults went tumbling over her lips, her eyes moving to look at Layton instead. "Have you ever deleted my memories?"

The question froze over the room. The heavy silence confirmed what she feared.

"Those were useless memories for you. I didn't take anything of any meaning. You saw something you weren't supposed to see." His voice was cold and monotone, somehow making his words sound even worse.

Her vision went red.

"How could you!?" Catherine hopped on her feet, fists clenched. "You had no right! Give them back!"

"I can't. And even if I could, I wouldn't." Layton looked down at her coldly. Did the man have any sense of feelings whatsoever? He was as emotional as a rock. And this riled her up even more. All things he had done to her so far had piled up and now spilling over the edge.

Her hand shot out on a whim. A loud clap of skin hitting skin echoed through the suite. Sharp stinging sensation rushed through her open palm that had just struck his cheek. "You really think you can just do whatever to people, don't you!? Pull them out of their lives, toss them about like rag dolls! I am not your marionette!" Catherine didn't bother to keep her voice down, didn't care for his reaction either. She had enough.

"It's thanks to you i'm dragged into this! You harassed me, took my memories! How about a 'sorry' you asshole!" Her voice broke. Tears gathered in her eyes, threatening to fall down her cheeks in salty trickles. She was slowly losing the fight to her overwhelming emotions.

Anger, sadness, confusion....She couldn't begin to count what she felt standing in front of the cruel man. If she kept looking at him for a second longer, she would collapse and break in front of him. She couldn't afford that to happen. Couldn't let him see her this weak, even if he already could get a glimpse of her pain.

Layton's eyes were wide open. He stood still, stunned, pain of her slap barely there. His focus was on her watery eyes. Those fierce blue eyes that always looked at him with such strength were now filling with tears. The last time she looked at him like that, he was pinning her to the bed.

He didn't move or say a word as the woman rushed off and slammed shut door to the bedroom. He watched her go, strange sensation spreading through him.

"You're such a ladies man..." Lucas murmured, emptying his glass in one go. "You have to admit....she is right."

Things were ought to get more complex. She knew who they were and now her life would be in even more danger. Catherine carried a secret she had no clue about and it would only be matter of time before she would find out why her soul was so precious, a wicked sin had set sights on her.

Chapter 20

S ilence hung heavy in the air. Pride had won the inner debate. She had made her grand speech and no curious question could force her lips to part. Her eyes found just about everything to be interesting as long as it wasn't the man she had to make the awkward flight back to Seattle with.

From time to time she felt his gaze land on her, burning her skin. At times she even caught glimpse of his lips parting as if he was about to say something, but no words ever came out. Both too stubborn to make the first step.

The flight attendants were careful around the two, offering drinks and snacks only from safe distance. The two poor ladies got their fare share of glares from both parties. Catherine could hardly blame them for being wary. Anyone with common sense could feel the bubble of anger building around them.

The car ride was equally awkward, only this time Layton didn't have a computer and his eyes were constantly on her.

"You can just dumb me on the next corner." Catherine finally spoke, hoping the driver would catch her words before Layton did. Another minute under his scrutinizing gaze and she would jump out of the car with little care of it stopping.

"That won't be necessary. You're going to live with me from now on."

"Huh?" There was a moment where Catherine's face washed blank with confusion, like her brain cogs couldn't turn fast enough to take in the information. "I ain't going to live with you-"

"You know too much. It's too dangerous for you to return to that rotten place." Layton explained calmly, silently savoring the moment before she went livid. "I already arranged your tings to be moved to my apartment."

Catherine was at lost for words. She had just processed everything she found out yesterday and now, her life had taken another turn! That man had no human side. He was a devil...a sin. Her life had performed a massive flip. There was nothing left from what she knew, all thanks to the handsome raven haired man sitting by her side.

Arguing was pointless. Inwardly she was screaming and yelling on top of her lungs, but all that came out was a long, tired sigh. She was exhausted from lack of sleep and overwhelming events. All night she spend pacing the room, thinking, fuming and panicking and now it was catching up. Her eyes were still puffy from crying. She felt helpless.

"Why am I even surprised..." She murmured, forehead pressing up against the cold window. The chill it offered cleared her head as more familiar streets of Seattle rushed b y.Towering homes of concrete created a grey blur that zinged past them. Somehow the view made it easier to disregard Layton's intense gaze. She felt him looking, not a single word exchanged until they finally stopped near an impressive sky-scraper in downtown.

The impressive building was similar to one Layton's office was located in, only this one was made for people to live in, a bit surprising that he needed that considering how much time he spent in the office.

Catherine trailed after the devilish man, taking in every curve of the apartment complex. It oozed luxury, endless rows of glass and steel shining in the evening sun.

Before long, she was presented with your cliche rich bachelor apartment. Clean, modern with very few personal belongings. Grey and black dominated the interior, clearly lacking woman's touch.

"Your room is upstairs."Layton instructed, tossing his suit jacket onto the leather couch.

"I am not sharing a bedroom with you." Catherine frowned, hesitant to take a step further than the front corridor.

"I have a guest bedroom. All your belongings should be there." Layton paused, giving her a long look. "Dress in something comfortable."

"Why?"

"There's something I want to show you."

Puzzled look crossed her features, her muscles not giving up the tension that had made home there since yesterday evening.

"Don't look so terrified." Layton sighed. "Just do as I say."

"Okay, okay. Don't be so bossy." Catherine grumbled, grumpy that the sweet dream of finally hitting the bed was fading away.

The room Layton had pointed her to was just as luxurious and empty as the rest of the flat, save for the pile of her stuff left onto the bed. It wasn't much.Some change of clothes and hygiene products. Though of someone digging through her underwear drawer had her cheeks pink.

These people have no sense of privacy.

She quickly washed her face and put on fresh clothes. Still far from looking like a decent human being, but this was the best she could do. Her overly pale skin and dark bags under her eyes could spook even a ghost back into the grave.

Layton was already waiting for her downstairs, dressed in a casual black t-shirt and pair of matching jeans. This was the first time she saw him wearing anything that wasn't a suit. His hair was slightly messy, having grown tad longer since the first time she met him. He looked like a hot bad boy you would see in Hollywood movies.

The steely gaze hadn't changed, though. After all this time, it was still hard to get used to his piecing sea blue eyes.

"Let's go."

Why his every word has to sound like an order?

"Where are we going?" Catherine questioned as they left the apartment, her tired self struggling to keep up with his fast pace.

"You'll see."

I have a bad feeling about this....

An elevator took them down to an underground parking lot. If someone stole all the cars parked there, they would be rich on instant. Just about every fancy car brand could be found there. Catherine couldn't help ogling at a black Ferrari they passed by. This was madness! How could people get that much money!?

"Stop staring and get in." Layton spoke up from behind her, making her flinch.

"Get in where?"

"The Ferrari you dumbass."

"It's yours?!" Catherine nearly shouted, not bothered by Layton's frown.

"Yes, it's mine. I wanted to go for something less flashy, but since you keep staring at it..."

Less flashy....that means he has more cars!?

"Can you even drive? I though people do it for you." Catherine circled the car, careful not touch it. God forbid she scratched it, no salary could possibly cover the expenses!

"It's only for work." Layton started the engine, mighty roar echoing through the parking lot. She barely had enough time to buckle up before he stomped on the gas pedal and sent the car flying down the narrow space.

I'm going to die young!

Catherine clung onto her seat as they sped away. The car swiftly cruised down the road,reflecting the setting sun.

"Slow down you maniac! Some of us aren't immortal!" The poor girl exclaimed, gripping onto her seat belt.

"I'm not immortal."

He just completely ignored my point!

A small smirk came onto his face, eyes sill fixed onto the road. Layton looked like he was enjoying himself and Catherine's screaming as well. He was purposely taking those corners faster than he should, her protests like music to his ears.

The air had been so heavy and now it seemed almost...playful. Eventually she got used to Layton's reckless driving. He still refused to tell her where they were going no matter how hard she pried. The sun had gone down when the car rolled to a stop, miles from city.

"We'll be there soon." Layton announced, getting out from the car. Catherine followed the suit,dubious. It wasn't everyday that she went on a road trip with a dangerous sin.

They were in some sort of park. It might've been pretty during the day, but in the dark it looked rather creepy. She quickly caught up to Layton up a small incline.

"Where is this exact-" She cut herself off. Her breath caught in her throat when a glamorous view of Seattle came in sight. From the hill they could see the entire city glow up in contrast of velvety darkness. Millions of lights reached as far as eye could see, glimmering and illuminating the ubiquitous buildings. It was stunning.

"Wow...." She sighed, amazed. "It's so beautiful."

"I know." Layton agreed. His expression was...gentler...than it usually was. Relaxed.

They took a seat on nearby bench, her eyes peeled on the scenery. "Do you come here often?"

"I come here to think." He replied, giving her a brief glance.

"It's a cool place to think. I had only my rotten apartment." Catherine chuckled bitterly, recalling how he had named the only place she could afford.

She was still mad, but in such a nice place she couldn't bring herself to think about it. For once she wanted some peace.

"I'm sorry."

Her eyes widened. Did she just hear things?

Did he just...apologize!?

"What did you just say?" A wide smile bloomed on her lips. So miracles did happen!

"You heard me. I won't repeat myself." Layton frowned, looking away from her. It could be the trick of her eyes, but she could've sworn his ears turned a shade of pink.

Catherine grinned ear to ear. She had just made Layton Grim blush.

Chapter 21

T ap...tap..tap...

Monotone sound of pen meeting the table filled the otherwise silent office. It tapped in a rhythm, composed by a very bored looking brunette. Catherine's blue eyes bore into random pile of papers. Endless sea of documents had tortured her for hours and for once she let her mind dwell on something that wasn't Layton's shopping bill.

A sin is not immortal, but can last without food or water for weeks. There are very few things that can kill them - That's what Layton had said on the night of their little trip. He had explained in detail how sins were stronger and in more than one way better than humans. Yeah....he was an arrogant peacock, but it had been the first genuine conversation the two have had.

He had apologized to her...It was just as unthinkable as putting a wolf and a bunny in the same room.

"Stop that." A dissatisfied voice loosely broke through the trail of her thoughts.

Tap...tap...tap...

"I said, stop."

Suddenly the pen was ripped from her hand. "Huh?" Catherine glanced confusingly down at her empty fingers, slowly regaining sense of reality.

"Did you even listen to what I say, Cavenon?" Layton's deep voice rung like a foghorn through her ears. Suddenly he had all of her attention. "Yes! I mean..no." She stumbled over the words, cringe coming onto her the very moment she realized how awkward she sounded.

"I did warn you not to space out during your work hours. You can play brain-dead when your shift is over."

"I dare you to say that again, mister! Actually, never mind, don't..." Se quickly corrected herself. Challenging him would only make her feel more offended by the end of the day. "So, what exactly did you say?" Catherine sat up straight in her chair. She was one of those people with the awful habit of sitting like she had no backbone and then regretting it later in the night when it suddenly turns out that she has one after all.

Layton gave her an annoyed look. That man hated repeating himself. "I said, contact my pilot. We will have to make a trip soon." He said, extra slowly.

"I am not brain dead!" Catherine snapped, instantly irritated.

"Really? Then don't act like it." The man shrugged, his gaze shifting back to computer screen.

And now he is dismissing me...

"Fine, will do. What trip is it?"

"One I don't want to attend, but hardly have any choice."

Wow, he's computer will crash if he keeps glaring at it like that.

Catherine knew better than to question him. Curiosity was killing her, but Layton looked to grumpy to respond half decently to anything. "Alrighhht...I will...go copy those papers or whatever." She quickly grabbed a random pile of documents from his desk. He needed them or not, who cares, her goal was to get out of the office before shit hit the fan.

Once the door shut behind her, Catherine breathed a sigh of relief. Finally out from that office. Ever since she found out about Layton, he refused to leave her alone. They lived together and he even moved her work station to his office! It was getting a bit insane...

I need a break from that man.

The young woman paused mid step when the phone in her pocket went off. Curious, she glanced at the screen. Nick's name came popping up, sparking some long absent joy.

"Nick!" She picked up without the second thought.

"Cat!? Fucking finally! I've been trying to reach you for a week! What the hell happened!?" The familiar voice came from the other end, bring a smile on her lips.

"It's a long story..." Honestly, she didn't know where to start explaining all the insane things that had happened to her.

"I bet it is, so you better tell me everything! Let's meet up at Joe's tonight."

"Yeah sure. I'll be there by eight."

"It's a deal, don't dare to disappear on me again or I'll set FBI on your tail!"

And with that he hung up, leaving her giddy with impatience. It had been too long since she last saw Nick. She was starting to miss him and the fun banter. Life was too complicated now. Even if she took out the ever irritated boss, it wouldn't ease the weight she had to carry. What better way to resolve this than by a drink and an old friend?

The hours dragged from the moment the short talk with Nick had ended. Catherine kept glancing at the clock every five minutes, curing the damn thing. Why does the time slow when you need it to go faster?

When it was finally six o'clock, she bolted from her seat, excitement rolling off of her in waves. "I'll be home later. Actually, I don't know if I'll be home, don't wait for me!" Catherine announced, her hand already reaching for the tattered leather jacket.

"Where are you going?" Layton's question made her pause. He had been so absorbed in work, she hoped he wouldn't notice her gone. Wrong. The man was sharp as nails.

"To meet an old friend."

"You're not going."

"Wha-Are you my fucking dad now!? I am going." Catherine rejoined.

"You're not. It's too dangerous." Layton turned his gaze to glare at her through his glasses, resolute to not let her leave. "There's a reason assassins are sent after you."

"Yeah? And what would that reason be?"

"You're an easy target."

"Bullshit." Her anger swelled. "I am going. I have a life of my own too and i'm going to live it. If you're so worried, you can come with me." Only second later did she fathomed what she had just said.

Oh, no.

"Very well." Layton nodded, satisfied with the compromise. He didn't bother addressing her facepalming in the corner. It had been her own idea after all.

"What happened to 'I will not concern myself with human business'"? Catherine performed the best Layton impression she could. She had screwed up, bit time.

"That was until you knew who I am. Now you're my weakness and I cannot allow anyone to use you against me." Layton explained calmly, pulling the glasses from his nicely shaped nose.

God, that was hot-Cat! Concentrate!

Catherine shook her head, all the best arguments she had tucked behind the belt already beaten. The young woman could only sigh in defeat and live with the mess she had caused.

"Did you really have to chose such a fancy car?" Catherine grumbled as Layton parked his brand new BMW near Joe's bar.

"I was not about to take a bus."

"You're too haughty for that."

"No, I'm too rich for that."

Catherine rolled her eyes at the self-satisfied smirk he sent her way. These rich people...I swear...

Getting out from the car, she could already see a familiar figure standing under the bright neon letters that read 'Joe's bar' in big bold letters. It was hard to miss the place. "Nick!" Catherine exclaimed, her engines kicking into motion.

She nearly tackled the tall man. "I fucking missed you!"

"Oh God, Cat. You're choking me!" Nick whispered, voice strained. She had him in vice grip yet he made no move to remove her arms from his neck. He was quick to return the hug, lifting the girl from her feet easily with joyous laugh. "You've gotten heavier."

"Did you just call me fat!?" Catherine gasped, not offended one bit. She was too skinny anyway.

Her smile disappeared when someone coughed behind them. Nick stiffened up as well, slowly lowering her to the ground. Layton stood wit his arms crossed over his chest, watching the two friends intensely.

I completely forgot about him....

"Uhm...Nick, this is Layton." Catherine introduced them awkwardly.

"Wait...that Layton?"

"Yes. That Layton."

"Oh...." Nick looked baffled, but being the professional side kick he was, the smile was quick to return. "Nice to meet you." He stretched out his arm for a shake.

All he got was a glare. Layton looked at Nick as if he was a scum. Catherine sent the black haired man an sharp look. He could do many things, but disrespecting her friends was not one of them!

As if reading her thoughts, Layton sighed. He squeezed Nick's hand in a firm shake. Very firm. "Layton. But I assume you already knew that."

He looks evil!

Layton was acting like a kid with his candy stolen. He had a dark, devious look in his eyes. For a second she worried for her friend's poor hand. When he finally let go, Nick's smile was obviously forced, mixing with slight pain.

He was quick to cover it up. "Let's go inside then?" Nick rubbed his aching hand, wry smile still lingering as he turned to enter the bar.

"Did you have to do that?" Catherine hissed, turning to Layton.

"Do what?" He looked down at her, innocently.

Fucking unbelievable! He is playing dumb!

Catherine's eyes narrowed, two fingers coming up to point at her eyes and then at him. "I'll be watching you." She warned, determined not to let him terrorize her friend.

There was no way she could survive the night with those two without getting wasted.

Chapter 22

"Another round!" Nick called out, waving over a curvy waitress. The bar was full that night. They barely got a booth to sit at. The woman was bustling around, cheeks red. This was all so familiar. Once she had been in that girl's place. There were only two waitresses for the entire bar and it was Friday. She felt sorry for the poor souls.

Layton sat besides Catherine, looking uncomfortable. He was squeezed into a corner he was obviously too hunky for. There was ever present scowl on his lips. Nick dodged the daggers thrown his way pretty well, each threatening look easily disregarded. Still, the handsome billionaire was making things awkward.

"Quit making a face as if you smelled something bad." Catherine scolded.

"But I did. It stinks like homeless man's breath here."

"I highly doubt I want to know how you know that and you're free to leave anytime."

"That's not happening." Layton glared at her, the blue eyes making the memo clear.

"Fine. Then quit acting like a snob." The young woman shrugged her shoulders, her attention turning back to Nick and the waitress that was setting down the second round of beers. She had missed the intoxicating kick of booze in her blood. It had been so long since she last had a drink that the first beer was already having an impact.

This felt nice...to let go and relax for once.

"You didn't finish explaining. So, you went to New York and then what?" Nick started up the conversation once the girl had rushed off.

"Oh, yeah. We went to this boring charity event or whatever. They fucking served snails." Catherine carried on, disregarding the strict look Layton was giving her. Once she learned to ignore his gaze the conversation flowed much smoother.

Empty glasses kept piling up on the table as the two friends talked. Nick shared the things that had happened during the time they hadn't met, slipping in a couple complaints about the old owner of the club she used to work for. The man was still an ass apparently.

Talking to Nick was always easy. He was a good listener and had just the right sense of humor to deal with the hyper woman across from him. They had clicked since day one.

"You should get a better job. You're a God behind the counter, at least find a place that pays decently."

"Looks who's talking. You can finally pay the rent with your salary, hm?" Nick chuckled, swiftly turning the topic back to her. Not that she blamed him for it. Neither felt comfortable with Mr. Scary around.

"She doesn't have to. She lives with me." Layton who had been silent most of this time suddenly spoke.

Nick choked on his beer. "She *cough* what?" The shocked man cleared his throat. "So you're like...together?"

"We are absolutely not!" Catherine panicked. Now it was her turn to glare at Layton. This had been the one thing she didn't want Nick to know and he blew it!

"Another long story, yeah?" Nick gave her a knowing look, teasing glint in his eyes.

"Yeah-"

"Hey, pretty." A drunken voice came from besides their booth. "You don't look like you're having fun. Join us." A man in his mid thirties slurred, his eyes glazed over by unlimited amounts of alcohol. The guy and his two wobbly sidekicks walked as if the ground was a deck of a storm-tossed boat. She had seen them looking, but hoped they wouldn't bother. How wrong she was...

"No thanks." Catherine dismissed them without a second glance. Years working for clubs worse than this one had her inured to drunkards and their attempts on flirting.

"C'mon...Don't play coy." The top dog of the group wheezed laughter, refusing to give up easily. "We could have way more fun together."

"Hey, piss off. Didn't you hear what she said?" Nick frowned, growing visibly vexed.

"And what ya going to do if we don't, pretty boy?" The men guffawed, exchanging glances. "We just want to have some fun-" One of them reached out to grab Catherine, eyes glossy with lust.

"I dare you to touch her, you pathetic scum."

The man froze up before he could touch her, his eyes now fixed on the looming figure behind Catherine. The drunk's face paled.

Layton stood tall. His eyes held a warning, he would not be above wiping the trio from the face of the earth. A single glance and he had the men stumbling back.

"Chill man, we mean no harm." The man grumbled curse words under his breath, wisely choosing to leave the woman be.

"Your boyfriend sure knows how to be intimidating." Nick commented, amused.

"He is not my boyfriend. Cut the crap." Her eyes turned to the still standing man. "I could've dealt with them myself."

"We're going." Layton said matter-of-factly.

"No, we're not."

"I am not asking for your opinion. We are going home."

"Hey! Let go!" Catherine protested, nearly spilling her drink when Layton seized her elbow and pulled her up with force. She bumped into his broad chest, her own legs like jelly after four beers. "Gimmie a break already! I am not done here."

"Tell that to those guys."

"They won't bother us-"

"Of course they won't, because we won't be here." Layton was not about to take no for an answer. Catherine glanced at Nick for help, but all she got was a concerned look in his eyes.

"Maybe it will be better that way. We can meet up again soon."

Unbelievable! He gave in!

"Betrayer." Utter defeat crossed her features. Not even Nick had the guts to oppose him. What a party pooper.

Layton produced a twenty dollar bill from his pocket, casually leaving it on top of the table. Without a single word he left the bar, dragging Catherine along by the elbow. "Let go, you're hurting me!" She exclaimed, struggling once the two were outside. His grip eased, but he made no move to release her completely until they reached the car.

"Get in."

"Will you stop barking orders! I am not your fucking lap dog!" The woman fumed, refusing to budge. In the chilly air her head felt a great deal fuzzier. Liquor swirled in her head, giving her the type of bravery that could only be described as stupidity. Alcohol made her want to defy the domineering man.

"Why are you in such a hurry? Are you jealous or something? That's it...isn't it. You're jealous of Nick and those three tipplers." Catherine laughed. "You are so selfish that you want me all to yourself."

"And what if it's true." Layton approached her again, staring down at her with those deep blue eyes, the usual chill in them present yet tinted with emotion she couldn't read. He had never looked at her like that....

"What if I want you all to myself."

Her laughter dyed down. Who was this man and what had he done to the arrogant boss she knew? He was so close she could feel his warm breath against her skin.

"You've been testing my patience too much, spitfire."

Catherine gasped. His arms suddenly wrapped firmly around her. In a quick motion he had her swept off her feet, one hand placed on her back and other curled under her legs. His muscles strained with her weight, pressing through the neat dress shirt. She barely had time to recover when he already had her placed in his car.

"If you need to puke, hold. I won't stand you junking up my car." Layton said. He leaned over, bucking the seat belt for her. His scent wafted over her with faint note of alcohol. He was completely sober, at least compared to her. A sin thing, she mused when the door on her side shut and he rounded the car to get into the driver's seat.

The ride was mostly silent and just as violent as the previous ones.

Does he ever release the gas pedal?

Her occasional complains about the evening ending so soon fell of deaf ears. He didn't even look at her until they were back into the safety of his apartment. It was dark and silent.

Catherine hadn't realized how much alcohol she had consumed. It was only now that the funny feelings begun to take effect.

"You didn't even let me say goodbye." She whined.

Layton had become her wall of support. The woman leaned heavily against him as he helped her up to her bedroom. "You smell good..." She murmured, burying her face in the crook of his neck.

"You're drunk. Not that I have to state the obvious. Go to sleep, we have some business to take care of tomorrow and

I won't be babysitting you then." He said, voice husky and oddly seductive to her ears.

Stupid alcohol...

It made the man seem all that more appealing.

"You're so mean. You treat me like I'm a unwanted child."

"I wouldn't if you didn't act the part." Layton sat her down on the bed, tired sigh escaping past his lips. This woman was such a hassle. But he couldn't bring himself to be mad.

"I don't understand why you don't just ditch me...like the rest of them." Catherine murmured, laying atop the soft mattress. the look in her eyes was distant, sad. "My parents didn't want me. Foster-parents didn't want me....So why do you do?" She gazed up at him, brave enough to expect an answer.

"I don't know." Layton sat down besides her. She reminded him of lost girl, pretending to be strong and fierce, but behind that mask hid a scared child seeking help.

"Will you...stay?"

The uttered words came as a shock for both of them. Her mouth moved before her brain did. It didn't matter, though .She wanted him to stay and her drunken state only helped to express that. Of all people, she desired the arrogant, rich bastard to comfort her. At least for one night.

"You're such a pain in the ass, Cavenon." Layton groaned, but he didn't leave. Instead, he leaned over her. "I don't think you realize what you just asked for."

His lips brushed hers. Not innocently, like a tease but hot, fiery, passionate and demanding.The world fell away with all rational thoughts. Her fingers slithered into his thick black hair, tugging lightly as he claimed her lips. His tongue intruded her mouth, meeting her own in a fight for dominance. The kiss was wet and needful, one that left the two of them breathless.

She wanted, no, needed more.

Chapter 23

The hot, messy kiss got her gasping for air when Layton finally pulled back. His eyes were darker, intent playing through his intense gaze.

"Just don't regret this, spitfire." He whispered in her ear, teeth tugging on her earlobe. Every heated breath had goosebumps spread across her skin. She couldn't even voice her answer when his lips met hers again, hungry.

Their breaths mingled, a rogue moan escaping in between their deep kisses when his hands begun to explore. His touch was expertise and far from gentle. With a deep growl, he moved both of her arms up, pinning them to the sheets as the other slid under her shirt.

The cold fingers made her flinch. Layton wasn't careful, he didn't feel around. Instead he went straight for her breasts. He played with the sensitive orb, pinching it between his thumb and index finger.

Catherine writhed, sensation causing her to produce another moan.

His lips had trailed down the path of her neck, sucking and licking with little care for marks left blooming on her skin. He was driving her crazy. Tingling sensation between her thighs intensified.

More...

Voice in the back of her head begged.

He released her arms from the vice grip, allowing some blood to flow into her hands.

Layton grabbed the edge of her shirt, pulling it over her head in a swift move. The piece of attire was tossed aside, followed by her bra. Her top was completely exposed to his intense touches and kisses.

"Spread your legs." He demanded.

Once she obeyed, he positioned himself between her thighs. His crotch pressed against hers. She felt the building bulge in his pants. His hips moved, tauntingly pressing against her though her jeans.

Layton's lower half rested against hers, as he held himself up by one arm. His teeth nipped on her nipple, hard enough to balance on the fine line of pleasure and pain. Wild shivers ran down her spine, her legs closing around his waist. Catherine was not a saint with her virginity intact. If there was a man who could taint her even more, it was him.

And she wanted him to ruin her....

His touch felt like something new, something she had been craving all her life, but hadn't experienced until now. She was not about to hold back either.

Her nimble fingers grasped the edge of his black shirt, dragging the fabric over the muscular upper body. Her nails scrapped against his skin lightly, urging him to get rid of the shirt. Which he did. With a low growl, Layton pulled it from his body. But he didn't toss it away.

Without warning, he pulled her up with him, once again taking a hold of her wrists. "Don't move." He ordered.

Catherine watched as he used the shirt to tie her wrists together. It only took him a moment before he pushed her back into the covers and once again got on top of her.

His lips were back on her chest, trailing down her flat stomach to the edge of her jeans. He wasn't stopping there. She could only blink before the denim was ruthlessly being pulled down her legs with her panties.

In a second he had her completely disarmed of clothing. Layton's steely blues scanned her body, taking it in. He didn't hide the sexual appetite that the woman had enlightened. She had tugged on monster's tail for too long, and now she would feel how it's like to tempt a sin.

His fingers caressed her inner thigh, hips still forcing her legs apart. Satisfied smirk came onto his lips when his fingers dragged along her opening. "You're wet."

Suddenly a finger pushed inside her cave, making Catherine's back arch. "Shit..." She cursed, trembling with the sensation of his finger thrusting inside of her. It felt good and would feel even better. Another finger joined the first one, messaging her.

He moved painfully slowly, teasing her. Still leaning over her, he observed her expression.

"Beg..." The demand rung clear.

"Nhh...No." Catherine refused, staring into his eyes with challenge.

His fingers stopped.

"Beg."

The young woman grit her teeth. She felt the pleasurable build up approaching. The lack of sex had made her extra sensitive. It was a painful choice between primal needs and her pride.

She hesitated, staring into his lustful eyes. He had an evil expression. He would be patient and ignore his own arousal just to torture her.

Slowly, his fingers curled to touch her g-spot. Another shock wave rushed through her, stronger than the previous ones.

"Well?" Layton grinned against her skin. "Beg...for what you want." He planted a gentle kiss on her lips, tugging on her bottom lip with his teeth.

All her resolve broke.

"Fuck me....please..."

Layton smirked, "Good girl."

His fingers slid out of her with a lingering touch as he got up. Catherine was left hanging, watching as he went to the nearest drawer and dug up a pack of condoms. Layton was back shortly, his hands forcing her legs open for him again. The zipper of his pants came undone, revealing a hard rod poking out from his underwear.

She felt her breath glitch. It was big.

Her arousal spiked up, anticipation killing her.

He let her watch as he revealed his manhood. The man didn't have anything to be ashamed about. She doubted he even knew what the word meant.

Layton positioned himself over her, his tip pressed against her entrance. "Tell me what you want me to do."

"You know, you jerk."

"Language." Layton pushed in, only the very tip widening her flesh. "Tell me."

He's a sadist!

"Fuck me already-" Catherine didn't get to finish that sentence, words replaced by a loud moan when he suddenly thrust his hips forward, entering her fully with a low groan. Her insides clung to his erection, pulsing.

"Fuck..." He growled a curse.

There was nothing holding him back. He rammed inside of her again and again. His hands dug into her hips painfully, holding her still against his hips.

Breathless gasps, moans and groans filled the bedroom. All thoughts lost to pleasure.

"God..." Catherine murmured between her desperate moans. She felt intense feeling building in her lower regions.

Her tied hands rested above her head. Every time she attempted to move them, Layton forced them back down. He had complete control over her.

The rapid thrusts didn't ease and soon orgasm hit her like a battering ram. Catherine's head fell back, her walls clenching Layton's erection fiercely. He slowed down, letting her ride out the overwhelming sensation.

She was pulsing and out of breath. Her body shook from the intensity. She felt herself growing limp underneath him, exhausted.

"I am not done yet." Layton flipped her around on her knees, pulling out to adjust her position, before he thrust inside again. Catherine nearly screamed. He had her insides raw and sensitive. He didn't give her any time to recover before his fast pace was back.

His low groans and rugged breaths rung in her ears as he leaned over to grasp one of her breasts. She could feel him throbbing inside of her, his own climax approaching.

Her eyes widened as he went even faster, low curses leaving his lips before he froze up, his entire body tense.

"Ugh..." He groaned.

She felt his manhood pulsate against her walls.

There was a moment of calm, both of them seemingly stuck in the position. Layton's breaths matched her own. Sweat beaded on their skin, serving as a proof of what they had done.

Layton pulled back with a low hiss. Without his warmth near her, she felt the chilly air of the room.

Shaky, she sat up, staring at her still tied hands. Her head was spinning, party due to the alcohol. She was exhausted. The pillow had never looked this attractive before.

I can't fucking believe it....I just fucked a devil.

Catherine collapsed back into the oft sheets, her eyes closing. She hardly payed attention to the shirt being removed from her wrists. She just wanted to sleep and never wake up.

Only the morning would reveal if this had been just a one night stand, their new game or a train wreck.

Chapter 24

A quiet groan came from underneath the thick duvet. It didn't take a genius to know that the person laying underneath was in pain. Bettering headache torture her poor skull, slight nausea adding to her misery. Catherine's brain felt like it would swell beyond the capacity of her skull.

"Kill...me..." The creature that was once a woman whined. Her eyes peeled open to the dimly lit room, though it is daytime no-one had opened the thick drapes.

Her mouth was dry and head felt fit to crack up any moment. Another groan rumbled through her chest. It was too fucking early to wake up. With a pull of her hand, Catherine snuggled into the covers. For a second she was peaceful.

A very short second.

The next moment her eyes were wide like five cent coins.

"Holy crap..." Hurriedly, she sat up. The room swayed wildly, nearly causing her to fall back. No fast moves when hangover, the basic rule she ad forgotten about. Once the bedroom became stationary again, her gaze settled on the blanket covering her body.

"Please no...please no..." Catherine uttered a quiet prayer to whatever God or Superman that was listening. The naive hope that it had all been a dream shattered as she raised the corner of the blanket. Her clothes were gone and she felt sore downstairs.

"I'm such an idiot."

"Agreed."

A deep voice coming from bathroom made all hair on the back of her neck stand. Slowly, she raised her eyes from her bare frame. Layton stood in the doorway, toothbrush in hand and nothing but a towel saving her from seeing him in all his naked glory.

He watched her with arrogant amusement in his eyes. Fresh droplets of water trickled down his rippled torso and the well defined v-cut. For a second she struggled to avert her gaze, the memories of the same body playing her in all the best possible ways came back to her.

"Did..did we..." Her groggy mind was seeking answers she already had. A small part of her still wanted to believe that she hadn't been dumb enough to hook up with a devil.

"We did."

Dang it.

"Oh my God..." She sighed, rubbing her face with her hands. This was bad!

"It wasn't God that made you scream last night." Layton smirked, watching her intently.

"Shut up. How drunk was I? Must've been pretty wasted to fuck someone like you." Catherine retorted, covering her chest with the blanket.

Layton scoffed, "Sober enough to beg for it." He returned to the bathroom, sound of running water echoing through the room.

The young woman felt her face turn tomato red with pure shame. if her head didn't already feel like a truck had ran over it, she would bang it against the nearest wall.

What the hell was I thinking!?

"Freshen up, we are leaving in an hour." Layton announced from somewhere in the bathroom.

Catherine frowned, "Where are we going?" The thought of going somewhere made her want to crawl into a deep black hole and not come out. The hangover was still knocking against her temple and her body felt as if she had fallen from three story house. Even making it down the stairs to get some water would prove to be a challenge. She would have to bump down the steps on her backside.

"We have an unpleasant event to attend." Layton explained, coming out from the bathroom already partly dressed. Still shirtless, he now stood before her only in his jeans.

"Nothing could beat the last terrible event." Catherine grumbled, slowly getting up from the bed. Her bare toes touched the cold ground, the sheet dragging behind her as she held it wrapped around her.

"Except for a family reunion." Layton said, not sounding too excited. His stare lingered on her figure. "You do know I've seen everything, right?"

"Doesn't matter. You ain't seeing any of that again." Catherine walked past him into the bathroom, still not quite realizing what a 'family reunion' could mean.

She had taken half a step onto the tiles when she felt something forcefully tug on the bed sheet. Her eyes widened as her only cover slid to the ground. "Shi-" Quickly her arms came to cover all her intimate parts as she swiveled around to glare at Layton who was casually holding onto the corner of her dignity.

"What did you say?" He asked teasingly, his eyes seizing her up. "Be ready in an hour." He then turned and left the bathroom with a deep chuckle.

Her cheeks burned. That man truly was the essence of evil!

The shower helped her to refresh and ease at least some of that pounding headache. Catherine was not certain how to act around Layton. It had just been sex, nothing else. It didn't mean she's special. It didn't mean he liked her any more than he did before...

Somehow those thoughts were painful. Did she want to be liked?

She shook her head, dismissing the annoying speech in her head. There was no forgetting what happened last night, her body was littered with evidence. Layton's hand prints were left behind on her hips and her neck was littered by hickeys. But she had to at least try to act normal.

It was just sex.

Once dressed and showered, Catherine walked downstairs. Layton was sipping on black coffee, his eyes fixed on computer screen.

"I swear, do you ever give it a rest?"

"My business doesn't stop when I get home. If I miss anything, it could cost me." The man answered, not even raising his eyes from the laptop.

"Spoken like a true Greed." Catherine rolled her eyes, casually strolling into the kitchen. She had gotten used to the place, already knew her way around some of the drawers and could operate the terribly complex remote that turned on the large TV and made the curtains move in the same time. Everything in this apartment was remote-controlled.

She opened the first drawer, eyebrows furrowed. Without painkillers, she was not leaving this flat.

"Advil is in the third to left." A deep voice boomed from the living room.

"Thanks..." Catherine murmured under her breath, slightly concerned if he could read her mind as well. Relieved, she finally dug up some painkillers. She had been so dumb as a kid, thinking that living in medieval ages would be fun. Who would cure her hangover without modern medicine!?

"So, this family reunion or whatever. I assume it won't be a warm family back-together." She mused, walking back into the living area with a chocolate bar in hand. Layton's fridge was empty as always, but she had managed to stumble upon his sweets drawer. Who knew he was a hoarder for chocolate, specially with peanuts.

"No. My father gets sentimental once a year. Our family is hosting annual auction. He wants to discuss details." Layton explained. His eyes landed on the chocolate in her hand, frown coming onto his features. "Where did you find that?"

"Hm? Oh this?" Catherine grinned, already tasting the sweet on her tongue. "In one of your drawers."

"Give it back." Layton demanded. His hand shot out to grab the bar. Thank God for her instincts. She stepped back before his large paw had snatched away her breakfast.

"What? No! I found it first!"

"It's mine and I'm pretty certain it's the last one. Give it back." Layton glared at her, shutting his laptop.

Oh-oh...he quit working, this is going to be serious.

"N-o." Catherine prolonged her answer, returning his glare. No would would take her God damn chocolate away.

"You will give it to me one way or another." Layton threatened, suddenly springing up from the couch and charging straight for the chocolate bar. The young woman had learned new ninja moves in couple of seconds, just to evade her chocolate from being stolen.

"Stop being so greedy! There's more chocolate in the drawer!" Catherine yelled, sprinting across the room with Layton hot on her heels.

"I want that one."

His massive frame suddenly crashed into hers, sending the two toppling onto the couch. A strained 'oof' escaped her lips when his weight landed on her much smaller figure. "You elephant, get off!" The woman hissed, arm stretched out as far as possible. She had worked too hard for the chocolate to give it up now.

All of her hard effort was in vain. Layton's tall frame had an advantage and before she knew it, he bit off a large chunk of her precious breakfast.

"Noo." Catherine whined. "You greedy monster."

The man smirked, full of himself. "You're too slow, spitfire."

"It wasn't fair, I'm hangover." She rejoined, pissed about her chocolate. Half of it was gone!

"If you want some, you will have to earn it." Layton said, swallowing the last bits of the stolen prize. Her frown deepened. The mischief in his eyes suggested that the 'earning' part was certainly not pleasant. The smug expression on his face made her hesitant to even ask. He was still towering over her, pressing her down onto the couch with his face close to her own.

Her mouth opened to voice a protest when another female voice interrupted her.

"Look at you two. How adorable."

The pair froze up. A tall, familiar brunette stood in middle of the living room. Sly smile played on her jungle red lips.

"Victoria..." Layton spat out her name like venom, his eyes settling into a brooding glare.

"Carry on, I didn't mean to interrupt the fun part." The woman grinned, easily disregarding the look her brother was giving her.

"How did you get into my apartment?" Layton growled, getting up from the compromising position the woman had found them in.

"You know, I have my ways." Victoria shrugged, her innocence as real as a mannequin. "You are growing attached to the little lamb, Avarice?"

"Don't be foolish, you venomous snake. What did you want?"

Catherine felt the temperature in the doom drop. Those two were scary. She didn't dare to move an inch, remaining sprawled across the couch with half of a chocolate bar still in hand.

"Rude." Victoria sighed, hardly surprised by the 'kind' treatment. "We live in the same city, I figure I'd step by and use your jet. It's a family reunion, after all. Wouldn't you want to help your little sister out?"

"No." Layton growled, his voice growing more stoic than angry.

"Boo. He's such a charmer, isn't he, little lamb?"

"My name is Catherine. Call me lamb again and I will make a pork out of you." Catherine fumed, sitting up straight. Layton's sister never failed to give her chills. Somehow she felt like a prey whenever the woman was around.

"Feisty, I like it."Victoria chuckled. "Is she coming with us?"

"She is." Layton confirmed, crabby as ever.

"Great! It's going to be so much fun. I assume she knows everything then." Victoria chirped, turning on her heel to leave the room. "Now, come you two. Father hates waiting."

Somehow I get a feeling, this is going to be one hell of a family reunion.

Chapter 25

The trip was miserable. Her hangover had lessened, but hadn't disappeared completely. The pressure from aircraft raising to the sky had her complexion turn green. And that wasn't even the worst part of it all. Layton was in a terrible mood and Victoria only made it worse. Her presents alone irritated the man beyond measure.

Catherine quickly learned that her sin was vanity and it couldn't suit her better. Victoria was like a bitchy female version of her brother. Some of the things she said on the ride got Catherine's hair to stand on end. At one point Layton even threatened to toss her out of the jet.

The flight wasn't long. Just over an hour later the trio were already sitting comfortably in a car, on their way to a lavish mansion.

With every mile passing beneath the wheels, Catherine felt her apprehensiveness escalate. She nervously gnawed on the insides of her cheeks and couldn't help her fingers from playing with the hem of her shirt.

By the time the car rolled to a stop in front of creaky iron gates, the nervousness had turned into dread. She could see an enormous building looming in the distance. It gave out a Victorian era kind of feel with large columns flanked on either side of dark wood door.

It would've been beautiful if she didn't know that the house hosted seven deadly sins and whoever their father might be!

"I can smell your fear, little lamb." Victoria spoke up next to her. "There's nothing to be so nervous about. It's just a friendly family gathering."

Something told Catherine not to trust the smile on the woman's face.

Friendly gathering my ass...

After a short moment the car was let through and parked in front of the mansion. They were greeted by lofty man and a couple maids. The female servants stood in a neat line by the door, their heads lowered. The butler also bowed when they got out from the car.

"Mr and Miss Grim. Welcome home." The man spoke in a calm, controlled manner. Catherine was fairly sure he saw her getting out from the car as well, but the man treated her like air.

We're off to a good start...

"Good to be back." Victoria smiled, taking in the large mansion before her. "Nothing has changed here. Say, are we the last ones to arrive?" She questioned the butler.

"I'm afraid so, Miss. Everyone has already gathered."

"I'm amazed. We came in after Sloth!"

"Enough. Let's get this over with." Layton interrupted his sister. He didn't bother to wait for anyone as he made his way up to the grand entrance. Catherine was quick to catch up. There was no way in hell she would leave the man's side anytime soon. He was her only chance of survival if things went south.

The house certainly didn't disappoint. The interior was just as glamorous as exterior. It oozed wealth and gave feeling that the owner of this house was alive way before she was even born. Wooden details mixed with crimson red fabrics. Wherever she looked, she could spot golden ornaments. Catherine already felt herself become overwhelmed. It felt like stepping into another century.

"Cavenon. Don't space out." Layton whispered in her ear, snapping her out from the daze. He couldn't guarantee her safety if she got lost.

"We hooked up and you're still calling me by my last name?"

All she got as a response was a glare. Of course. One night hadn't changed a damn. The thought sent pang of through her chest. Somehow it was painful to think that.

Catherine shook her head, quickly getting rid of those thoughts as she trailed after the two sins and the elitist butler. They were lead into a grand dinner hall with a long table placed in middle. Some of the seats were already taken.

All people present in the room looked over at the new-comers. An elderly man sat on the end of the table. He was Layton's lookalike, only older. His black hair and beard were mostly papered with grey and his face was littered with wrinkles, but he had the same, pale blue eyes that could piece through flesh with single glance.

The young woman sucked in a deep breath. The air felt heavy, in a way she couldn't quite explain. She felt like a mouse that had stumbled upon lions den.

Her soul nearly jumped from her body when the butler shut the door behind them with a loud bang, trapping her with seven sins.

"Father!" Victoria was first to speak, her lips stretching into a Joker like grin. "You haven't changed a bit-" She was silenced by a raise of his hand.

They say that no matter how many times you look into the eyes of fear, you will never get used to it. You will always bend your knee and succumb to it's overwhelming force. Some do it in a way which forces the ground below them to break, some just slightly bend their knees out of pride. It doesn't matter what the case, fear is fear. In her case, she could only slightly bent her knees and hold her head high when the elder man looked straight at her.

"So you must be the one..." Layton's father spoke. His voice withheld the same authority and power as his son's. Apple certainly hadn't gotten far from the tree. "I didn't expect you to bring along human, Avarice." His father's hand remained raised, keeping his son from answering.

"Pardon my manners, young lady. What is your name?"

"Catherine." Her voice leaked hesitation. The young woman barely managed a brave face. So many different colored eyes bore into her with mix of different emotions, most ranging from disdain to disgust.

"Catherine." Her name rolled over the old man's lips as if he was savoring the taste of it. "That's a strong name, I like it. Come, I want you to sit next to me."

"Father! That disgrace has no right to sit besides you!" A young man stood abruptly from his seat, furious. His vivid green eyes shone dangerously as he glared at the human woman.

"Silence, Envy!" The order froze over the room. "Sit down, or leave my sights!"

"I apologize, father." Envy bowed his head, quietly sitting back down. One look at the man and it was clear that she was just a pest to him, someone not worthy of even licking his shoes.

Catherine glanced up at Layton, her eyes seeking out his in a silent plea. She did not want to be here, but hardly had the choice. He simply nodded, urging her to do his father's bidding.

Why does it have to be me in this mess!?

After all of them had finally taken a seat, the tension lifted somewhat. Layton sat besides her as a wall between her and the other sins. Victoria got a place on the other end of the table besides a man Catherine was already all too familiar with.

Lucas winked her way suggestively. Nothing ever bothered him and there was always one thing on his mind. He wasn't Lust for nothing, she supposed.

"My name is Rikard, as you know, these are my children. I would like to say you have met all of them, but Sloth once again has lost interest in all family matters. You might find him sleeping somewhere at a later point." The man introduced himself. His tone chilled to bone, even if he spoke politely. "May I assume that you are...familiar...with our situation?" Rikard glanced at his son as if to ask if he had explained things to her.

Layton nodded, his mien one of stone.

Rikard gave a wry smile of approval, "Good." His eyes rested on the young woman for a moment longer, considering. "But she hasn't realized it yet, huh."

Catherine frowned. "Realized what?"

I am getting sick of this family talking in riddles.

"No, nevermind. I was talking myself." Rikard waved his hand dismissively. "Let's move on, you all must be hungry."

On a cue, the ample, two sided door opened again, revealing line of servants. Each carried a silver platter with some sort of meal. Delicious aroma filled the room. A part of her was surprised to see appetizing looking food set in front of her instead of some high end delicacy that was hardly edible.

Her stomach groaned happily. Having eaten only half a chocolate bar, she was certainly hungry.

"Catherine," Rikard addressed her once the meal had begun, "Out of curiosity, do you have any idea who I am?"

Catherine paused mid chew. The gears in her mind begun to turn. She had zero clue. "Satan?" The first possible option tumbled over her lips, causing the imposing man to chuckle loudly.

"So, I was right about you! You truly are an interesting...pe rson." Rikard noted, amused. "No, my dear. I am just a demon, but I've heard the Satan is quite an impressive man."

Well, that doesn't make it any less creepy.

"Father, you're being too obnoxious." If there was a man that could talk like that to Rikard, it was Layton. The two exchanged a long look. The inner fight between father and son was rather obvious even if no words were spoken.

Rikard was first to break the silence, "My apologies. I did not mean to bother you with such questions."

"It's fine.." Catherine murmured, impressed by Layton. Everyone in the room, even usually bubbly Victoria and Lucas were wary of their father and yet he spoke freely against him.

The meal carried on, muted conversations exchanged among the sins. She could feel eyes on her at all times, glares and stares of interest. Both equally unsettling. Layton looked unapproachable, but she felt him looking as well, like he was trying to protect her with his gaze.

His family wasn't one of seven angels. He would never admit it or say it out loud, but he was possessive of the woman sitting by his side. She was his and none of his siblings would have her.

As the last course was being served, Rikard once again spoke to his children. "I would like to hear the newest details of auction." His tone had gotten serious, demanding.

Auction....I hear that word an awful lot lately...

"Father, do you really believe it's a wise decision to discuss this in front of a human woman?" A man who had been silent all this evening spoke. A man..that description didn't quite fit. He looked more like a human shaped pudding. He had twice the amount of food on his plate and he didn't even empty his mouth before speaking.

"Perhaps you're right, Gluttony." Rikard turned to Catherine. "My dear, would you mind? We have some important things to discuss and I'm afraid they will bore you to death."

They could just tell me to get lost.

"Yeah, alright." The protests were pushed down her throat. The odds weren't exactly in her favor. She wanted to stay and hear what this auction was all about, but there were other ways to find out without pissing off some powerful demon and his seven offsprings.

Layton caught her wrist when Catherine made a move to leave the table. "Don't wader off. Stay by the door."

"Whatever you say, boss." She spat the words, clearly not satisfied by him ordering her around. This event was staring to suck, real bad.

The door slammed shut behind her the second she left, the thick wood forbidding a single word from reaching her ears.

Catherine sighed, defeated.

They didn't even let me have a dessert....

Grumpy, she took a long look around. She found nothing of interest in the spooky house, when suddenly her eyes stopped on slightly opened door down the hall. "Oh..."

Layton had made it clear that she was not to go anywhere. Smart idea would be to listen....but that wasn't the exciting option.

She was in the house of sinners, might as well sin a bit.

Chapter 26

Stealthily the young woman approached the opened door. She felt like Indiana Jones, sneaking into some forbidden place for treasure. Her breath remained trapped in her lungs as she leaned in to peek through the narrow gap.

What she saw, wasn't what she had expected. No monsters jumped out from shadows and this was no secret torture room either. She had stumbled upon a library.

Talking about disappointment....

This was a house that belonged to a powerful demon, a creature that shouldn't even exist and the best thing she could find was some old library!? Really!?

Her shoulders slumped, all hope for finding anything worth of interest, gone. Nonetheless, she was banished from the elite meeting and she had nothing to do. She was not about sit by the door and wait for her master like a lost puppy.

The door cracked open, inviting the woman into the dimly lit library. Row after row of neatly lined up books with their spines facing outward were placed on floor-to-ceiling shelves. There wasn't a single speck of dust anywhere. This place was well cared for. It owned a certain smell of an aged paper and leather. Most of the books there were old with yellowed pages and smears between the chapters.

"Cool..." Catherine approached one of the shelves, running her fingers along the thick covers. Her gaze stopped on a certain book. Bible.

Ironic....Bible in devil's home.

She bit her lip, fingers itching to pull the book from it's designated place. Maybe some of the answers she had were hiding there.

"So it's true."

Catherine nearly jumped when a male voice came from somewhere behind her. She whipped around, startled, expecting to see Layton or worse - his dad. But no one was there. Her eyes landed on red leather couches positioned in middle of the library.

"Excuse me?" Slowly, she approached the red couches.

"I was surprised at first, but it's true. My brother has taken in a human toy." The same boyish voice came from behind the couch. Catherine glanced over the cushioned back. A man with platinum blonde hair was laying horizontally across one of the couches, his eyes closed and earbuds blasting music.

"First, I am no ones toy, I'm a person! And second, don't you know it's bad to give people a fucking heart attack!?"

The man opened his eyes, an eerie shade of pale grey. "And don't you know that it's bad to snoop around?" He retorted.

"I wasn't snooping around. I was just trying to pass some time. They kicked me out from their fancy family gathering."

"Sounds about right...." The man sat up, his eyes narrowed as if the poor lightening was burning his colorless eyes. "Father will be angry," He murmured to himself.

"Let me guess, you're Sloth." Catherine noted, observing the sleepy man.

He didn't grace her with an answer, not that it was not needed. His appearance spoke for itself. Everybody in this family were devilishly good looking and terrible. The teenage boy on the couch was no exception to this observation.

Maybe except that Gluttony guy, he was just terrible.

"You're bothering me." The man grumbled.

"That's your problem, not mine."

"Leave."

Catherine folded her arms, "No."

"I was here first."

"I don't care."

The sin groaned, "You're so annoying." Brushing back his platinum blonde hair, he slowly stood up. "I am starting to understand...why my brother keeps you around." He looked over at the persistent woman. "It's not because he likes you."

Catherine felt prickling pain in her chest. She knew Layton possessed no feelings for her and yet hearing that hurt. "Yea? Then why do you think he keeps me around?" She kept her stance.

Sloth slowly approached. He wasn't taller than her, and was rather scrawny by built. Aside from his creepy eye color, there was nothing in him that could intimidate her. He was just a teenager.

"Your soul." The man grinned, now standing inches from her. Catherine took a step back, bumping into the back of the couch. "It smells good...I'm pretty certain you're the reason they're holding that meeting in the first place." Sloth closed the distance between them again, trapping her between him and the couch. He inhaled deeply, smirking. "I could just take it for myself-"

"I thought I told you not to wander off."

Catherine turned her head to the side, leaning as far as she could from the blonde sin. Layton stood in the doorway. Judging by the taut tone of his voice and sharp look in his eyes, he was moderately pissed.

"Finally...came to pick up your toy? I was getting annoyed by her." Sloth stepped back, his expression changing to one of boredom.

"I said, I'm not a fucking toy! What's wrong with you people!" The woman bit back angrily. This 'toy' thing was seriously starting to paw at her nerves.

Layton advanced towards her, giving her a cold look. "What part of 'stay by the door', you didn't understand?"

"I was bored. You can't just leave me and expect me to act like an obedient slave!"

The man sighed, giving up on the fight. "At least you're not hurt." He murmured, his eyes softening somewhat.

"You were worried?" Her eyebrows raised with curiosity, voice dropping to a teasing purr.

Layton scoffed. "Don't be foolish. If something happened to you, it would be a nuisance I would have to deal with, that's all." He didn't look her in the eyes as he spoke.

Cute.

The young woman grinned, seeing straight through his lie. "Just admit it, you were worried." She bumped his side with her elbow, earning herself a warning look from the hunky sin.

"You should keep a better eye on your toys, brother. Or you might lose them." Sloth spoke, lazily sauntering back to the couch.

That guy, I swear!

"Ignore him." Layton took a hold of Catherine's arm, leading her away before she had the chance to roll up her sleeves and punch out the blonde's teeth.

He took her to a sumptuous bedroom. Like everything else in the mansion, it looked like it belonged in antique store. Large king size bed was placed in middle, ruby red covers neatly tucked around the cloud-like mattress. Curtains hung from poles attached to a detailed wooden frame, giving it a historical vibe. The luxury of this place never failed to impress.

"You're going to stay with me tonight." Layton announced, making himself comfortable in one of the armchairs. He looked like a king sitting in a throne, calmly gazing at the peasant that had come to him.

"No, thanks. This mansion has enough rooms for both of us."

"It wasn't a request, spitfire. It's not safe for you to stay alone, besides, it won't be the first time we share a bed." He looked at her smugly, eyes traveling up and down her body. "You're quite clingy during the night."

Her face flamed. Unfortunately she was not one of those people with talent to hold back a blush. "That's a lie." Catherine huffed stubbornly. "And would it kill you to call me by my name!?"

"No."

Her lips tugged into a scowl. "Fine...whatever." She grumbled, walking up to a glass door that lead out to a balcony. The room offered a beautiful view to thick forest stretching ahead, faint light of sun dipping down caressing the three tops. "What is that auction about?" The question had been on the tip of her tongue for a while now, bugging her.

"It's none of your business." Layton's tone of voice suggested he would not be answering that question, but she was not about to give up either. She had to know.

"Boo hoo. Wrong. Somehow, I get a feeling that it is. I hear about it all the damn time." Catherine turned to look at the devilishly handsome man, her arms crossed in bold refusal to let the question go. She was like a bulldog with a bone, once her teeth had sunken into the topic, there was no letting go. "I am human, but I am not dumb."

Layton stared at her in silence. She refused to budge. His glare no longer had the effect on her.

Finally, he caved in, "Every year my family hosts an auction for sins and powerful demons." He begun to explain, "Our powers require a source to seek strength from. That source are human souls."

Her heart dropped to her stomach. "You sell humans?" She had been suspecting some illegal shit, but not auctioning off humans!

"Their souls." Layton corrected her.

"And that makes it okay!?"

"Keep you voice down." The man reprimanded, his voice a low growl. "This is going on before you or me. My world is different from yours, that's why most humans don't know about it. Sins and demons exist in shadows. Without us your world wouldn't be as it is. Those souls die quickly and painlessly, if that comforts you."

"It does not." Catherine felt a sudden need to sit down. "What about....my soul?" Her chest clenched. Did he plan on selling her off as well?

"What about it?"

"Did you plan on selling it?" Her gaze held his, the air around them thickening with tension.

A moment of silence passed before Layton finally responded, "No."

That's a relief.

Her shoulders slumped, as she relaxed. She couldn't be sure if she could fully trust his words, but something told her that he wasn't lying. Or so she hoped...

Eating human souls. That explained the hungry looks and odd comments she got from other sins. Their, 'you smell good' never failed to give her creeps. Now she knew, they saw her as their daily burger.

"Is there something else I have to know about your world before I hear it from someone else?" Catherine questioned. He certainly wasn't telling her everything.

"No. You already know too much. The more you ask, the more I put your life in danger." Layton stared at her intently, almost as if he cared.

She shook her head. Of course he didn't care. It was just her stupid brain coming up with something she secretly wanted. "I will worry about my own life." Catherine sat down in an armchair across from the raven haired man. "Let's play a game." She suggested, "You tell me what I want to know and in return, I will tell you something you want to know."

He will never agree....Why would he want to know anything about me?

Layton remained silent, his long fingers caressing his sharp jawline in deep thought. The cold blue eyes never left her, observing if her determination would drop. It didn't.

After a very heavy second, he finally answered.

"Deal."

Chapter 27

The air was so brittle it could snap. This was her chance to get answers and all she could do was sit there and stare fixedly at the sea deep eyes of the sin. She was awestruck that he had agreed so easily.

The soft armchair hugged her figure in an almost distracting way. Not that the piece of furniture was to blame. Her buzzing mind found just about anything distracting now.

"Will you ask the question or you will keep eyeballing me?" His eyebrow cocked in amusement.

Catherine frowned, barely holding back a snap. She couldn't lose this chance to her temper. Shaking her head, she jerked back from her restless thoughts. "Jeez, give me a minute to formulate it."

"You're so slow."

"Shut up." The woman shifted in her seat, nervous. "How do you eat souls?" The question terrified her more than the answer. It sounded sick, insane. The words fell from her lips clumsily, like ones of a child speaking for the first time.

Layton chuckled, having already predicted the question. "That's really what you want to know?"

"Just answer."

"It's called 'kiss of death'. We take the human's last breath." He explained calmly. His stoic face unsettled her. They were talking about killing people like taking a stroll in the park. "People sold in the auction are chosen very carefully. Their souls are marked."

"How are they marked?"

"Those are two questions." Layton pointed out. His sinewy upper body leaned forwards as he rested his elbows on his knees. "My turn." The position made him look bulkier than he was and for a split second her mind trailed off to places she didn't want it to go. The shirt curled tightly around his bulging biceps. It was enough to distract anyone, honestly.

"Back then, why did you steal my wallet?"

Catherine was slightly taken aback. "That's a stupid question. You were being an asshole!"

That much is obvious, duah...

"That's not what I meant. You had other reasons, didn't you?" His captivating eyes didn't allow her to dodge this easily.

She swallowed a none existent lump that had formed in her throat. "I was broke as shit. I needed money for rent. I am not some rich kid who's only worry is to buy a new Lamborghini. I'm an orphan, life ain't easy for a street rat."

Layton looked thoughtful, like he had more to ask. He was actually curious of her. "Your turn." He said after a bit, his gaze tracking her every move.

"Did you grow up in this house?"

That was random.

She couldn't help it. Catherine wanted to know more about sins and souls, but she also wanted to know more about him.

"No. I grew up with my mother." He looked to the side, offering her a brief moment of relief. For once she was not pinned down by the intensity of his gaze. "She was a beautiful and a stingy woman."

"Was?"

"She's no longer in my life."

Catherine bit her lip. She couldn't sympathise, she didn't have parents in the first place, nor had she ever truly lost someone she cared about. But she couldn't bring herself to just sit there like a log. Slowly, she stood up from the comfort of the armchair and approached him.

His expression remained stony, but there was a glimpse of pain behind his blue eyes, one he refused to express openly.

Her smaller hand traveled over his in the best attempt at comfort she could muster. "I'm sorry." She was not good at this and was sure this sounded just as awkward as it felt. None of the emotions she felt were fake, though. She really wanted to make him feel better.

Layton scoffed as he tore his hand away from hers. "Don't be. I brought it upon her." He looked at her, cold smirk on his lips. "You don't know anything about me. I don't need your pity." She stumbled back when he suddenly stood up, his six foot tall frame easily towering over hers.

"I was not pitying you!" Catherine stood tall, not intimidated by his sudden outburst. They were quite similar when it came to being defensive. "Look, I might not get how it is to lose a parent and I am sorry about that, but I don't pity you. I envy you." She stopped, realizing what she had just said.

The taller man looked down at her, the wrath replaced by cat-like interest. "Envy me?"

"I didn't....mean to say that." Catherine groaned.

"Too late, explain." Layton demanded, folding his arms as he waited for her answer.

She felt put on the spot. Like a cornered animal, her eyes scanned her surroundings for a way out, only to find none. Her heartbeat picked up. He had caught her off guard and now the sky--high walls were beginning to crumble.

"You have everything I don't. Money, power, decent childhood." Catherine begun, "I have never had that. Other kids got home to return to, I had my drug dealer as a lover." She laughed bitterly.

"I'm envious because the only luxury I had, was another dose and bad romance with a sick man who was only using me." The words poured from her lips before she could stop them. Tears begun to form in her eyes despite her attempt at stopping them. Her hands balled into taunt fists, her head lowered to avoid looking at him.

Silence settled among the two. It was heavy, torturous. She felt ashamed. If the ground opened and swallowed her, she would be thankful.

I'm such an idiot...I shouldn't have said anything...He doesn't care. he will laugh-

Her thoughts were silenced by sudden warmth enveloping her. Suddenly, her face was buried in broad chest and a comforting hand rested on the back of her head. Long fingers traced the loose strands gently. Layton's strong arms held her in firm embrace. It spoke louder than words ever could.

Her heart performed a back flip, butterflies exploding in her stomach. Slowly, her hands raised, wrapping around him. Perhaps she was being clingy, but she didn't care. All that mattered was his warmth and delicate caress.

Layton's chin rested on the top of her head, his eyes closed. They were like fire and ice. She was his spitfire. Stubborn, foul mouthed and possibly the only woman capable of yelling at him. At first it had been annoying, but now, he preferred that over the pained look on her face.

There was no telling how long the two remained frozen, lost to each others touch. It could be a second or an hour before Layton broke the silence.

"I erased my mother's memories...." He murmured, his voice a low whisper. "She was lost to sin, devastated by my father's actions. It was better for her not to know, to start over. She was suffering with her child having born as a sin."

Catherine pulled away slightly to look into his eyes.

"She was stained by me and I don't want to do the same to you." His hand brushed back her hair, caressing her cheek like it was a delicate flower.

"You won't stain me....because you can't stain something that's already ruined."

His hand drifted to her hip. It settled there and pulled her closer. Catherine inhaled sharply. She was against his warm chest, chiseled to perfection. Their breaths mingled as their faces grew closer. With the first brush of his lips, her eyelids dropped closer. She allowed his kiss to consume her.

She had tried,but she couldn't deny it anymore. Somehow, feelings had bloomed and they were stronger than anything she had ever felt.

At first, it was a delicate butterfly of a kiss. Then, his arms encircled her. He drew her to him, the kiss now demanding of more. She hardly had a moment to react before he pressed his tongue to the seam of her lips and, at her grant of access, delved inside her mouth.

Catherine moaned into the passionate kiss, her head spinning out of control. She no longer could hold the snowball from rolling down the hill. She was in too deep.

Layton bent down, suddenly lifting her up. Her legs wrapped around his waist, her lower body sitting comfortably on his hips. His lips were back on her lips, trailing down her chin and nuzzling into her neck.

He carried her effortlessly to the bed, her legs on either side of him, straddling his lap. Layton caught her lower lip between his teeth, tugging and nipping between their hot, messy kisses as the two sat on the edge of the mattress, her still on top. His eyes snapped open, focusing on hers in the split second of pause, clearly displaying his ravenous and growing desire for her.

"You need to find a new lover." He whispered huskily in her ear, sending wild shivers down her spine.

This was not enough. More...

Their hands worked to undo each others clothes. It didn't go smoothly and way slower than desired, but neither of them cared. Neither were satisfied until their naked skin touched. And even then it wasn't enough.

Her hips had a mind of their own as they begun to move against his hardened erection impatiently. The friction drove her insane with lust, feeling his bulge against her sex.

Layton did not need more ushering. His strong arms wrapped around her to flip them over, when she suddenly stopped him. "I want to be on the top."

He paused, looking a tad taken aback before a devilish smirk sneaked up on his lips. "Alright, spitfire. Ride me until morning." He grinned, laying back against the mattress wit his hands still on her hips.

"You wish." Catherine barely held back a smirk of her own. Her hand slipped into his boxers, delicate fingers wrapping around his shaft. Layton groaned with her practiced movements. The muscles on his core tightened every time her hand encircled his massive tip.

Sweet, sweet revenge.

"Beg." She demanded, evil glimmer in her deep blue eyes.

His eyes peeled open, glaring at her. "Spitfire....you're playing a dangerous game."

"You want me? Then beg." Her grip on his shaft tightened, movements slowing. Layton growled lowly with the sensation.

"Don't fucking mess with me, woman."

"You mean like this?" Her fingers ran across his tip again, her thumb rubbing against the top teasingly.

"Fuck-"

An animal like snarl rumbled through Layton's chest as he sat back up, dark look in his eyes. "What happens next, you brought it on yourself, spitfire." He gave her a wicked look, one that didn't suggest anything good.

Shit!

The young woman was quickly ripped from her throne of dominance. Before she could blink, she was pinned to the sheets by Layton's powerful frame. With a swift thrust he spread apart her lower lips and entered her body.

His moves were ruthless, fast and hard. Sound of skin slapping against skin filled the room, mixing with their sounds of pleasure.

That night, no matter how much she came and begged for him to stop, he didn't, until she passed out underneath him out of pure exhaustion.

The next morning came with odd sourness through her entire body. Catherine woke up feeling fatigued. The sun had already climbed the sky by the time she forced her eyes to open. She was alone, the spot in bed besides her cold. Layton had left some time ago.

We did it again....What the hell is going on with me?

The woman groaned. Her body begged to stay cuddled up under the covers, but her mind was uneasy and she really needed to go to the bathroom. Eventually, the bladder won the fight and she got up. Throwing on a pair of jeans and a t-shit, she quietly exited the bedroom with mission to find the nearest toilet.

The mansion was gigantic and her precise sense of direction failed her rather quickly. After five whole minutes, she was still wandering around in desperate search.

Fuck, fuck, fuck. This is the worst!

"Greed said he won't be attending the auction. What nonsense is that!?"

Catherine halted at a voice coming from other end of wooden door she had just passed. Pausing, she took a step back. Eavesdropping some secret conversations hadn't been her goal, but who could resist? Making sure no one was around, she pressed her ear to the door.

"Obviously, he already snatched a special soul for himself. Why would he?" She recognized Lucas's voice, tad muffled by thickness of the wood.

"That's selfish."

"Don't be so jealous, Envy. You're just grumpy because you didn't find her first."

"I must admit, though. The whole love act is very impressive coming from him. Poor, naive little lamb." Feminine voice joined the conversation. It was Victoria. "He will steal her soul on the night of full moon and grow in power. He has been very patient with her. We have to give him more credit."

Steal my soul?

Her heart dropped. Betrayal spread through her body like poison.

He's been planning on killing me all this time....

The young woman stumbled back, pain grasping her chest. She had trusted him!

I'm so fucking dumb...

She couldn't begin to wrap her head around this. What was she supposed to do now? She couldn't stay knowing he would suck her soul out!

I have to get away.

Chapter 28

R un.

The word had been ringing in her ears since they left the mansion. It was damn hard not to flee around the nearest corner and she would've done it, if it wasn't for the wise voice in the back of her head that whispered for her to wait for the right time.

So, there she sat stiffly in Layton's office chair, waiting for him to finish an angry phone call. His voice boomed through the room, scaring away every single employee that passed by. It was Sunday and yet the office buzzed with people. They had been gone for one day and so many things had gone South without the man's supervision.

"You all are bunch of ignorant fools!" He roared into the phone before hanging up. His hand shook with rage. The man was seconds away from flinging the device across the room. "Fucking idiots. They screw it all up!" He continued, making the secretary standing in the corner flinch with dread.

Angelique had entered five minutes ago and her boss hadn't even noticed her.

"What's wrong with you?" Layton's sharp tone sudden-ly addressed Catherine who had been sinking in her own thoughts all this time.

"Huh? Uh, nothing." Her gaze lifted from her lap for the briefest moment. She didn't dare looking him in the eyes. They were like a reminder of who he was and how he had used her. It was painful.

"Don't lie to me." He growled. "You haven't said anything since we got back. Don't be a nuisance and tell me."

The woman glared up at him, "I said it's nothing. Go do...s ome stuff."

The room froze over with the way his eyes narrowed at her. "Cavenon," His voice held warning. "I won't repeat myself."

"Nobody's asking you to." Catherine shrugged, seemingly unbothered. The flight back had been long and awkward. She was silent the entire way, quite a massive change since yesterday when she had been the one demanding answers.

A loud 'crack' echoed through the room as the expensive smartphone cracked under Layton's fingers. This was the first time they had a chance to talk. All the time he was bombarded by phone calls and dozens of questions. This someone that had messed up, had done Catherine a huge favor.

"Uhm, sir?" Angelique, a.k.a, the blonde bimbo, squeaked from the corner, finally mustering enough courage to speak.

"What?!" Layton's roar sent the woman stepping back as if he was a wild animal preparing for attack.

"The partners are holding an emergency meeting...They're waiting for you."

The man sighed tiredly, dismissing his secretary with a quick wave. "I'll be right there." His eyes once again landed on Catherine. The woman swiveled in his chair, not bothered by his anger. The first chance she got, she would be outta here and never see him again.

"I'll tell the driver to take you home. We will talk when I get back." His eyes remained fixed on her for a second longer, like he wanted to stay more, but no words came. Layton left the office in couple swift strides.

The second the door shut behind him, Catherine hopped up from the leather chair, her heart sent into overdrive.

Fucking finally.

She had waited for hours. The words of sins still rung through her head. She had been a fool to let herself be charmed by a sin.

I should've done this long ago.

Catherine made sure Layton was nowhere in sight before she left the office building. As promised, the car was already waiting for her, but she was not about to head back to his apartment. She might not get a chance like this again. The stuff could be replaced. There was only one place she could think of where she would feel safe.

The young woman made sure no one saw her, that no one followed her, before she set into a sprint down the street. Luck was on her side this time. She managed to grab the last bus that would take her back to the scraps she came from. Fancy life was never hers to have in the first place.

Only when she slumped into the uncomfortable chair besides some old, smelly hag, did she breath a sigh of relief.

Soon Layton will find out that she's missing. She had two hours at the best.

Catherine shook her head. No. She was not going to dwell on him. That jerk was in the past.

It took her little over an hour until she stumbled upon a familiar apartment in a run down building. Her feet brought her to old wooden door, her knuckles rapping against the messy red paint that was starting to peel off at places.

Muffled grumbling, followed by footsteps came from the other side. The door opened moments later, revealing a familiar dark eyed man.

"Cat!?" Nick's eyes widened in surprise, the beer nearly falling from his hand. "What the fuck are you doing here?"

"Hi, I need a place to crash." She forced on a smile. While she was happy to see her friend, the situation was seriously starting to weigh down on her.

"Sure, umm, come in." The man stepped out of the way, holding the the door open for her. "What happened? Got into a fight with your rich boyfriend or somethin'?"

"He ain't by boyfriend!" Catherine snapped, "But yeah, I guess you could say so...." She couldn't really tell him what was the real reason behind her escape. He wouldn't believe her in million years.

"Did that dick do something to you?" Nick growled, the door slumming shut. "You say a word, and I'll punch his teeth out."

"No. It's...complicated.."

The young man frowned, giving his friend a concerned look. "This is not like you." He sat down besides her on the old couch. "You can talk to me ya know. I didn't trust that guy from the start."

"Yea, yea. I just need a place to stay." Catherine murmured, snatching the beer from his hand.

"Hey-Give that back." Nick exclaimed, his hand shooting out to take the beer back with little success. He was quick to give up. After couple exchanged curses, he could only sigh and sit back. "Why do you always bump into bad guys? I mean, seriously. You have some bad karma, girl. First Jace, and now this Layton dude."

"Don't fucking ask me." Catherine chuckled bitterly, taking a sit from the stolen drink. Bitter taste filled her mouth with a light fizz. Cold beer...nothing could beat that after a hard day. Or week, in her case. Her insides churned at the two male names. Both were nightmare in her life. Both of them equally evil.

Jace....He had abused her for years and she had been too young and naive to realize until the night he violated her and revealed his true nature. She had just barely escaped him. He was sick...Like a beast with his eyes set on deer, he had chased her until she moved to Seattle.

Catherine shook those thoughts away. Now she had another predator on her tail, perhaps more dangerous than the previous one.

"I will leave first thing in the morning..."

"Where will you go? You can stay here for a while." Nick offered, frown etched on his face.

"I can't. He will find me eventually. I can't put you in danger."

"Like hell. He won't stand a chance against me." He growled, angry. "I will beat him to a fucking plump if he'll do something. That mafiozo better not show his ugly mug here."

"Chill man." Catherine chuckled. Nick was a nice guy, one of the rare ones, but he also had bar-fight personality. She could already imagine how bad their meeting would end. If Layton wasn't a sin, she would actually fear for him. "I have a plan, don't worry." She lied.

I don't have a fucking clue what i'm going to do...

Nick watched his friend, nut brown eyes full with suspicion. Only after a bit he gave up. "Fine. You better. Just know, you can stay here whenever."

"I know....thanks." Catherine smiled.

Their conversation went off on a more casual note from there. Nick didn't press, even if the lingering concern in his dark eyes was still evident. The man clearly made an effort not to interrogate her.

They talked for what seemed to be for forever until she begun to doze off, half empty beer bottle still in hand. A soft groan rumbled through her chest when Nick dropped a blanket over her figure and took the bottle away from her stiff fingers.

Tens of missed calls glowed on the screen of her phone, gone ignored along with dozen of unread messages from the man she had recently escaped from. They all consisted of the same ting. 'Where are you!?' 'Cavenon, pick up your phone!' 'I'm coming to pick you up!'

None of them mattered anymore to the sleeping woman.

"Night...." He murmured, pressing a gentle kiss on the crown of her head. Nick didn't get much response to that. The girl was out cold on his couch. The man took a moment to look over her sleeping figure.

He had always found her beautiful. She was not your ordinary girl. Her walls were built sky-high, but underneath she was kind. Innocent.

"I almost feel bad for doing this to you....I'm sorry." He murmured. The time had come. After all these years, it was so close, he could taste it.

Nick leaned over, producing a small bottle from the pocket of his sweatpants. His other hand came over pinch her nose. As her lips parted, he brought the small bottle to her mouth. The transparent, sour tasting liquid trickled past her lips. It's abhorrent taste filled her mouth, making her eyes snap open with shock.

The initial reaction made her want to spit it out, but before she could, a large hand clasped in front of her mouth.

"Shh...shhh....You'll be alright. Swallow." Nick whispered, holding her firmly. His hands blocked all oxygen from entering her body.

Catherine's eyes were wide in horror, her legs kicking the blanket from her body as she struggled. Her hands gripped on Nick's arms in a weak attempt to rip the off of her. She couldn't last long. Her body forced the unknown liquid down her throat. It burned, feverish warmth spreading through her.

"Good girl." He murmured when she swallowed, finally releasing her.

"Nick....why." Everything was blurry. Darkness pressed in, her consciousness fading rapidly.

"I'm sorry." She heard man that was once her friend utter before she succumbed to blankness.

Everything was dark. She was alone, trapped in her own body. The time was blurred. She didn't know where she was or what was happening. When her heavy eyes opened again, everything was still dark like she had gone blind.

Panic gripped her in it's steel hold. She couldn't move her body. She couldn't even breath without struggle. Even if she wanted to scream, nothing would come out. Her limbs didn't listen and her throat felt sandpaper dry.

She had been through many things worthy of heart attack, but she had never been this frightened. The fear shook her to core, waves of heat and terror washing over her as a familiar voice broke through the darkness. A voice she couldn't forget even if she tried. A voice of fear itself.

"We finally meet again."

Chapter 29

"How long has it been? Two years? Three? Do you even remember?" The voice spoke from somewhere in darkness. Low and threateningly sweet. It was a familiar timbre, one that awoke deep rooted dread. "You were asleep for so long, I got worried." Footsteps approached her, slow and taunting.

The darkness was suddenly replaced by faint light as the sable fabric bag was ripped from her head. Catherine blinked, her eyes taking their time to adjust. She found herself in a basement lit by a single light bulb. It offered just enough light to reveal three men present in the room. Two of them she knew very well.

"Don't be a jerk, Jace." Nick sat in the corner, his arms crossed over his chest and a deep scowl on his face.

"I would never be, watch your tongue, boy. This is my lady. I would never wrong her." Jace, a dark haired man, purred. He had changed since she last met him. His once powerful build was now gaunt. He looked like a man that had seen the worst and somehow had survived. Hollow-cheeked and grizzle; he no longer could charm a woman to his bed.

His demeanour hadn't changed thought.

"I wanted some chat time before we close the deal, but you, my dear, were out for so long, we don't have a whole lot left. Pity." He smirked, leaning down to the same eye level as Catherine. She was bound to a metallic chair, her hands tied behind her back firmly. She could only watch as his hand caressed her cheek. "Did you miss me?"

"Fuck you." She spat, glaring at the man the best she could.

"Ah! You haven't changed at all! Still as fiery as ever, even after we...broke up." He chuckled, grasping her chin painfully. "Sad, I was hoping you would be at least a little submissive. Our fun night taught you nothing."

"Nick....why?" Catherine stared up at Jace, forced to look at him, but she did not want to talk to him.

"I'm sorry, Cat. It had to be done." Nick's voice filled the basement. "I told you about my mother. I need money to help her. This will be a new start for me and her."

Betrayal darkened her eyes. Nick's mother was gravely sick. The young woman knew that, but nothing could justify his actions. She really was alone in this world. Layton had used her, Jace had used her and Nick as well....her only friend. "You knew this from the start?"

"Don't fucking ignore me!" Jack interrupted, squeezing her cheeks. "I am here as well. I recruited him, I was the one that payed him to find you!" Jack snarled, his grip on her tightening. "It took me years to get to this moment." He spat out every word, his chest heaving.

"Jace. Client said that she has to be unharmed." A third man she had never seen before spoke. He had been silent, watching the scene unfold with his back leaned against the door. The guy was so casual, like he was waiting for coffee in Starbucks instead of watching someone being abducted.

Jace took a deep breath, chuckling as he exhaled. "You're right. I got carried away." He released Catherine's chin, giving her an amused look.

"It's just been a while. These meetings are always emotional." He took a step back. "As I begun to explain. I hired Nick. He sure was silent for a long time," Jace glared at the said man before carrying on, "But life always sets things right. I have found myself other girls to play with, you were without a doubt my favorite, but times change. I just wanted to see you one more time, and so it happens, that I also get a good cash out of it. Two bird with one shot. I get to see you pay for leaving me, and I get money. Fair, right?"

"You're a sick man." Catherine growled, wrath mixing into her voice. "You will be the one regretting this."

"Uff, i'm scared. And what will you do, hm?" He taunted, giving her a hungry look.

"Wait until I get out." She said through gritted teeth.

"How could you do this to me!? I trusted you!" Her head snapped to the other man, one person she had trusted and considered close.

"It's nothing personal. I liked you, I really did. But my mother needs help and I can't let this chance slip. I'm truly sorry, Cat." The brown eyed man didn't even look at her. Nick kept staring at his shoes. She could see his regret, but it was too late now.

"Don't call me that." Catherine shook her head, the pain in her chest growing with each word. Tears were starting to spill over without her consent. Her fingers curled into fists behind her back. Life was merciless.

"Alrighty, enough chit chat. I'm sure you two have a lot to discuss, but we have to get going. We can't miss the auction."

Her figure stiffened at Jace's words.

An auction?

"You have got to be kidding me....You will sell me!?" Her attempt at keeping her voice fierce failed. She nearly choked on her words.

The disgusting smirk on her kidnapper's face got her gut twisting. "Yes. And I will watch every moment of your misery, my dear." Jace snapped his fingers, glancing at Nick as he pointed towards his hostage. "Get her prepared, we're out in ten."

"Don't you dare to come near me you fucker." Catherine growled when her ex-friend stood up. His face held no emotions. He didn't look her in the eyes, ashamed of what he had done. "I'm really sorry. I don't expect you to forgive me, but I need this money. I don't want to hurt you, so please don't resist."

Her teeth grit together with enough force to shatter. "You've got to be shitting me." Her legs kicked up as Nick came to stand in front of her, sending a swift kick to his gut. The man doubled over, taking a couple steps back. The hit hadn't been strong enough to do much damage though.

"Cat, don't do this. I will have to sedate you." He straightened up, hand lingering on the place she had hit.

"Nick, hurry up, or you won't get your cut." Jace called out from behind him, urging the man to be quicker.

"You don't have to do this." Desperation sneaked into her speech. "We can find other ways to help your mom."

"It's too late. She doesn't have more time. This is the only way I can help her before it's too late." This time she was too slow to react as he moved behind her. "I'm sorry." Nick murmured again, producing the same bottled liquid from his pocket.

"Nick-Don't!" She was cut off by a hand clasped over her mouth and nose. Catherine screamed into his open palm, her blue eyes wide with horror as the bottle was brought to her lips. She moved her head from one side to the other to avoid drinking the odd sedative. It's odor and taste were unpleasant,made her feel sick.

"Don't give her too much. We want her conscious during the auction." Jace instructed as Nick forced the bottle to her lips, his strong arms holding her head still and her nose blocked. Her hands tugged frantically on her restrains and her legs kicked the air in a feeble attempt to knock over the chair and set herself free.

Useless.

It was all useless.

Out of breath, she was forced to swallow the liquid. The second her lips parted for wisp of air, it was rushed into her mouth and down her throat. The same burning sensation started up again. Nick stepped back as she gasped, holding onto the last bits of fading consciousness.

No, no, no!

Her brain quickly became a mush. She didn't completely pass out, but the room around her blurred and the voice was men around her morphed into distant noise. She suddenly didn't have any strength in her bones. Her own heartbeat droned in her ears as Nick untied her jelly-like hands.

"Let's go...Big cash is waiting for us." Jace beamed, not bothering to mask his excitement. Nick had enough decency to stay quiet to that as he supported Catherine's delicate body. Her one arm hanged limply over his broad shoulders, her head turned downwards and eyes party closed. The third man in the room came up from the other side, catching her other arm.

The way out from the basement and up dozens of steps went by in a daze. Jace wouldn't shut up. His dirty compliments and degrading words hardly reached her ears though. That was the good side of whatever drug they had given her.

The three men lead her into a room, similar to a backstage. More people crowded there, none of them looking even slightly disturbed by the girl that was dragged along by the kidnappers. All of them wore vintage masks, their identities hidden.

A voice of a host speaking excitedly into a microphone came from somewhere above them, but she couldn't make out the words.

Catherine was taken to a barred bird cage set on a small podium. Nick gently helped her sit down. "You will feel better soon, I promise." He murmured, giving the woman one last glance before the metallic door was locked behind him.

Her head lolled to the side, resting against the cold iron bars. Through fog, she watched her three abductors be approached by one of the masked people. The man was tall and thin, oddly familiar in a way, but she couldn't recall where she had seen him.

"I thought I made it clear that she has to be unharmed!" He shouted, pointing an accusing finger at the caged victim.

"We ran into a bit of struggle with her, but I can guarantee that she's alright. She's just a bit dizzy, 'is all." Jace explained, wry smile on his lips. "We would like our cut."

The masked man scoffed, "You will get it when the auction is over and she is officially mine."

"That was not out deal-Ghu!" Jace was interrupted by a fierce hand wrapping around his throat. "How dare you speak to me like that, you human scum!?"

Human scum?

Catherine's eyes narrowed, focusing more on the man. She had certainly seen him before. Only people that talked like this were sins....

Oh God.

Her breath hitched. It was Envy!

That means this auction....is for souls!

Her heart dropped to her feet. The realization instantly sobered her up. At least as far as her mind went. Her body was still weak as she clutched the bars. "Nick...." She called out weakly. "Nick! You have to get my out! They will kill me!" Her voice cracked. That stupid drug was making her unable to fight or even attempt to escape.

Nick didn't even glance over at her, his attention solely on the two arguing men.

"M-my apologies. We'll wait." Jace managed the grunt out between desperate gasps for air. Envy hesitated to let go, savoring the power a moment longer before finally releasing the man's throat.

"Out of my sight. I will give you your cut later." He waved them off dismissively.

"Nick! You have to help me!" Catherine tugged on the bars as if her weak body could make them budge. This time the man did look at her, but it was already too late.

The mechanisms underneath the podium came to life, slowly lifting it up towards an opening in the ceiling.

"Shit....Nick-" Catherine was silenced by sudden blinding spotlights searing into her eyes.

The sight she was presented with damn near got her heart stopping. She was on a huge stage, hundreds of people sitting in front of her, all wearing fancy ball gowns and masks.

"Soul number 25!" A host spoke into microphone, huge smile on his lips. "The starting price is two million! Who will be the first bidder!?"

Chapter 30

"Three million and a half!"

"Four million!"

"Do I hear Four million and half!?"

The host shouted, scanning the crowd for bidders. The numbers skyrocketed, more and more people joining the bid. Catherine could only watch helplessly as hands holding a sign with number raised one after another.

"Six million! Is someone bidding more, Yes! Number 559 bids seven million!" If she wasn't being sold off like some antique garbage, Catherine would actually be impressed by how fast the host spoke.

"Is there someone bidding more than seven million?!" The man paused, searching the crowd. No numbers raised. "Seven million once! Seven million twice! Seven million-"

Another man suddenly rushed up on the stage with a phone in hand. He handed the device to the host before he could say the final bid. The host paused, taking the phone.

His menacing grin grew.

"We have the highest bid. Ten million!" He announced after handing the phone back to his assistant.

Catherine's head spun with the violently growing numbers. Her fear escalated when the man turned back to microphone. "Ten million once! Ten million twice! Ten million thrice! Sold!"

"I object! You can't do that!" She yelled, but no one payed any heed to her protest. Two more men walked up on the stage, heading towards her cage. Her grip on the bars tightened as the door opened.

"Let go!" She screamed as the two strangers grabbed her by her arms, dragging her out from the cage. Catherine dug her heels into the stage floor, fighting against them the best she could. The drug was still coursing through her blood. Every time she tried to pull away, her head begun to swim.

She had given the two a hard time removing her from the stage, but that served as little comfort when she was dragged behind the scenes and further down a hallway.

"Someone help!" Her cry had no response other then a rough tug from one of the men. He huffed out a curt 'shut up' and carried on with his job.She was lead up a flight of stairs into another hallway. Her yelling was ignored as the two pushed her inside a room.

It was a luxurious lounge with black leather couches and ruby red walls. The type of setting one could find in fancy sports bars. A crystal chandelier hanged from the ceiling, casting it's light over the otherwise poorly lit room. A man sat like a king in a leather armchair, his legs crossed and arms settled on the padded armrests.

Catherine raised her eyes from the lush carpet covering the tiled floor, resting her gaze on familiar icy blues. Her stomach dropped. In the make-shift throne sat the very same man she had recently escaped from.

"Would it kill you to listen to me for once, spitfire?" Layton spoke, threateningly calmly. His voice could freeze hell over.

Her eyes narrowed, "It would, actually! I know what you planned on doing! Either way I would've ended up on that stage!" She fought not to totter on her unsteady matchstick legs. Her body begged for her to put her butt on one of the chairs, but her stubborn brain much rather have her faint than approach the dangerous man.

"And where did you get that information from?"

"I heard your siblings talk. They made it pretty clear that you will suck out my soul." Her fists clenched. She wanted to take her heels in hand and run for her dear life instead of having this conversation with him. But she had no clue where she was and how far she would get with the masked creeps hanging around on every corner.

Layton sighed, his legs slowly uncrossing. "Did you now?" He stood up, straightening his suit jacket of any wrinkles with a sharp tug. "And you believed them?"

Catherine stepped back as he slowly advanced towards her. With every stride he took closer to her, she stepped back until her back bumped into a wall, trapping her. "Give me a reason not to!"

"I did not plan on attending this auction. I am here only because you can't keep yourself away from trouble, Cavenon." He closed in, coming to stand inches from her. She could smell his fresh scent, feel his body warmth without them even touching. His gaze felt heavy on her, pinning her in place.

Why did this man had to be devilishly handsome even when she hated him!?

"Why would you care if I got into trouble? You will kill me. You had no reason to attend because you already had me close." The words pouring past her lips were painful to her own ears. A part of her wanted to believe that there was something between them. That he was not just manipulating with her to gain power. That she wasn't just a chess piece in his game.

Layton was silent, staring down at her coldly. The seconds ticked by like hours as they held the staring contest. It confirmed her fear. Her pulse picked up.

He's going wipe me from the face of Earth....

As the thought passed through her head, Layton grasped her hand, pulling her behind him in a swift move. She had no time to question or scream as the door suddenly swung open with a loud bang of the doorknob digging into the wall.

"Greed!" Furious Envy rushed into the lounge, his face red and green eyes raging. He looked like one man Christmas tree, the Krampus version. "Her soul is mine! I demand you to give her back!" He roared, chest heaving with pure wrath.

"It is not." Layton countered calmly, his bigger hand still wrapped around hers as he kept her hidden behind his broad back. "I won the auction. She is sold to me not you."

Envy grit his teeth, his puffed out cheeks turning an even deeper shade of ruby. "You were not supposed to be here."

"Yes, until you chose to take what's mine."

The green eyed man growled, his irises glowing up. "Greedy as always. Her soul was mine to have. I will have her back one way or another."

"No." Layton's grip on her wrist tightened, his eyes withholding a piercing glare. "She will not be taken by anyone. Do I need to remind you of consequences if you attempt to take her by force? Father won't be forgiving."

Her heart pounded inside her chest. She couldn't see the other man, but she was fairly certain he looked as infuriated as he sounded. Layton on the other hand was calm as a cucumber, not even slightly disturbed by the peeved off sin.

"You fucking bastard-"

"He's right." A feminine voice cut in. Victoria leaned against the doorway, slender fingers toying with her mask. "You tried hard, brother, but she's out of your reach. Rules apply for everyone."

She sauntered inside the lounge, smirking. "Oh, and you forgot your goons." With a snap of fingers Jace, Nick and the guy she didn't know name of were dragged inside by three masked men. "We already expected you to play dirty, but for you to go this far....I didn't know you have it in you."

"You set me up! I want my money!" Jace roared, struggling fervently to get loose from the two men holding him. He had gone berserk, twisting his body in near every possible position just to get lose. His wide eyes rested on the sin that had betrayed him, expecting an answer. But...

Envy ignored him, not caring one bit about some low life human. His fists were clenched and he looked ready to destroy the entire building and whoever it contained. The man would not come in terms with his loss anytime soon. His brother outsmarted him and nothing could be done.

Catherine locked eyes with Nick, not caring much for others. He instantly averted his gaze. The man couldn't even look at her anymore. He was left without money or his friend and only had himself to blame.

What a coward.

"What are we going to do with them? Lust suggested feeding them to demons." Victoria addressed Layton, staring wickedly at the three men. "I could give them a taste of their own poison. The auction is not over. Their souls aren't anything special, but someone will buy them."

"Feed them off, I don't care." Layton spoke, cruel glimmer in his eyes.

"Wait!" Catherine shook off his grip on her hand, stepping forwards. "I don't care what you do to Jace and the other dude, but leave Nick be."

Everyone looked stunned at the request. Nick glanced up from the ground for the first time, shocked. "Cat...why?"

Layton frowned. "Yes, Why?" He questioned, his arms coming up to fold in front of his muscular chest.

"Don't expect me to forgive you. I don't ever wan to see your face again. You will live with what you did and regret it until your last breath." She stared into Nick's eyes, hate boiling into her own. Betrayal stung, badly. She knew him for years, and therefor also knew that he's not all bad, just desperate. This would be a way more severe punishment than any other.

"Uhh. Dramatic. I like her." Victoria interjected. "Alright then, escort the friend of the year out and put the other two up for auction. Let's hope someone will find fun in torturing such a dark soul."

"You can't! Let go! I want my money!" Jace raved. He screamed and fought as he was hauled out from the lounge with the other man. His voice echoed through the hallway even after he couldn't be seen anymore. Nick paused, locking eyes with the woman he used to call a friend. "I'm sorry-"

"Go. I don't want to hear it." Catherine looked away, her gaze fixed to the ground until the door closed behind him. She knew she wouldn't see him again, but the hurt would linger no matter how much time passed.

How can I trust anyone anymore?

Victoria's voice brought her back to reality, "I believe you two have a lot to talk about." She addressed Layton and Catherine when only then sins were left in the lounge. "I'll deal with our little mischief." She winked towards the other woman before giving the overly silent Envy a pointed look.

Layton nodded, glancing down at Catherine. "Let's go."

"No. I'm not going anywhere with you." She stepped back, putting some distance between the two. The woman was so caught up with the drama that she had completely forgotten the real problem here.

He sighed, "Give me a chance to explain myself."

"Why!? What could be your excuse for wanting my soul!?"

"I don't want it."

Catherine paused, her prepared speech flying right out of the window. "Huh?"

"Come with me, I'll explain once it's only the two of us." Layton looked down at her. He was a pro liar, but she couldn't spot the darkness behind his gaze that came with untruthful words.

The inner battle showed on her face.

To be or not to be? To go or not to go?

After a long moment of silence, Catherine finally gave in. "Fine. But if you try anything funny, I swear to God, I will be the worst thing you have come across." She threatened.

Layton released a breathy scoff. "I don't doubt that."

"Come on you two. Get a room already. I don't want to see the rest." Victoria spoke up, urging them to leave.

It was a fairly silent trip through the lorn hotel, reserved solely for the event. The tension built up to near unbearable by the time Layton lead her into one of the suites. The door closed behind him, leaving the two alone in the dark room.

"So....you don't want it?" Catherine was first to break the silence, still keeping a safe distance from the sin. "Answer honestly. I am sick of bullshit."

"No." Layton replied, his eyes resting on her. "At first I saw you as a toy. I wanted to sell you, gain money. Then, I wanted your soul for myself when I realized you're special." He slowly approached. "But now...I want you, not your soul." He came to stand a short distance from her. Layton had to crane his neck to look her in the eyes, his taller built easily towering over her.

It was distracting, the way he stared down at her. She had to gather all her will power not to bend underneath the intensity of his gaze. Her heart raced, this time not out of fear.

If this carries on, I'll age sixty years in one day.

"And...your point is?"

"You've changed me...." He whispered. "You're possibly the only human capable of seducing a sin." He took a hold of her arms, his thumbs rubbing gentle circles on the back of her hand. "You make me...feel something."

Sparks went flying. Trusting a sin was like borrowing money from mafia. It was perilous and plain out stupid. And in this case...irresistible. "Are you trying to tell me that I'm special?" Catherine grinned, teasing tone waving through her words.

Layton rolled his eyes, mildly annoyed. "Don't get cocky."

"Or what?"

"Or this..." He suddenly bent down, sweeping of off her feet in a gliding motion. Catherine gasped, the ground ripped from underneath her. The pressure of wall went up against her back as he pinned her between him and the structure. His face was so close, she felt the feathery touch of his breath.

With their lips inches apart, she was tempted to close the distance completely, to feel his skin against her own. Her hips sat comfortably at his navel, legs wrapped around his waist. Catherine's fingers found their way into his jet black hair.

"Catherine...."

Her eyes widened.

Did he just call me by my first name?

The way her name rolled off his tongue sent wild shivers down her spine. "Say that again."

"No." He smirked, finally leaning in and pressing his lips to her own. Instantly her body was overwhelmed by wave of heat rushing through her. The kiss took her breath away, his mouth moving against hers, his tongue teasingly caressing her own.

The kiss became deeper, more passionate. All thoughts were lost, until he suddenly pulled away, an evil look in his eyes. "You still have to pay me back."

"What?" Catherine blinked, out of breath.

"You owe me ten million."

"WHAT!?"

Chapter 31

"I won't pay you a damn!" Catherine exclaimed, pushing against his chest with all her might.

Useless, the bulk didn't budge.

"Yes you will," Layton smirked, looking like a true devil. "You will pay me with your body."

Her stomach flipped, breath caught in her throat as his hips thrust forward. "I still have to punish you for running away from me."

"I-it was your fault to begin with-mmmh!" He silenced her with another kiss.

"You will do ten things, each worth a million." He whispered against her lips. She felt his sinister grin. "First thing, you will strip." He suddenly let her go, stepping back to give her some space. His hungry blues rested on her body, making her feel naked before any layer of clothing had even come off.

"I won't!" Catherine protested, her cheeks set aflame.

"Would you rather prefer me doing it for you?"

"No!"

With a slight shake in her hands, Catherine begun to take off her leather jacket. It fell to her feet, followed by the two beaten sneakers and her t-shirt. He had seen her naked before, but somehow this felt different. She was that much more exposed to him emotionally.

The jeans slipped off her slender legs, leaving her only in her underwear. "There. Done!"

Layton's eyes had darkened with lust. He scanned her body from head to toe, arrogant grin on his face. "All of it." He ordered.

Catherine stiffened up, giving him the best glare she could manage. Nevertheless, she obeyed. The bra went flying to the nearest armchair and her panties fell on her jeans. The moisture had begun to form between her lower lips from his eyes and demands alone. The man never failed to flip all the right switches in her mind.

"Good girl." He growled out, a bulge already forming in his dress pants. "Now, undress me."

She hesitated, pushing back the feeling of vulnerability. He was making love to her with his gaze. Her skin felt hot, tingly. Layton made no move to touch her, he only watched as she begun to unbutton his jacket, vest and finally his white shirt. Firm abs were exposed to her with every button that came undone.

Catherine bit her lip, tempted to touch the tan skin, but he caught her wrist when she tried. "Not yet." He lowered her hand to his belt. "Carry on."

She swallowed, seeing the hard rod sticking out from his pants. A bit clumsily, she undid his belt and the fly.

"You're cruel." She grumbled, the tingling on her lower parts intense.

"I know." Layton said proudly. "Now, Turn around and bend over. Don't move no matter what I do." He instructed, waiting for her to obey.

Catherine did as told. Her arms rested on the back of an armchair. Finally he would satisfy her needs, ease the wild sparks between her legs.

Or so she thought.

The touch never came though. She felt him shift behind her. Rustling of clothes being disregarded could be heard along with his heavy breaths. The young woman barely resisted glancing over her shoulder to see what he was doing.

The answer came soon enough as an open palm smacked against her bare ass. "Fuck!" Catherine flinched, more out of surprise than pain.

"Don't move." Layton pushed her back when she made a move to turn around. Another slap came, this time harder. She bit down her arm, the sweet torment serving to turn her on even more.

"You've been a bad girl,"

Slap.

"You escaped me."

Slap.

"And you made me worried." Another spank came, this one more gentle than the rest of them. Her rear had gone red, aching from his merciless hand.

"I made you worried?" Odd warmth filled her chest at the words. It wasn't lustful kind, it was just warm...

"I'm not repeating that."

"Come on, please-"

"Stay down." Layton growled when she attempted to twist around again. "Spread your cheeks."

"That's too much-" Her protest was cut off by another loud slap.

"Do it."

The woman sighed, moving her arms to grasp her rear, her chest propped on the armchair in a rather uncomfortable position. Her face felt hot and furiously red, but her fingertips freezing against her own skin.

Layton grunted, turned on by the sight before him. She was held up by dizzying suspension, unable to see what he was doing. But then she felt it; his long fingers running up and down her slit. One entered, pushing against her tight walls.

Catherine moaned as his digit turned and moved inside her, painfully slowly. His thumb messaged her clit, his touch could barely be felt.

Torture.

"M-more." She breathed.

"Not yet." He was enjoying this, his voice a low purr.

That sadist!

"P-please."

"No."

She whined as the movement suddenly stopped, just as her buildup had begun. "Turn around." He ordered, and she did. Layton was fully naked, his pride standing tall, throbbing with anticipation. The rippled muscles of his stomach clenched with need as he pushed her back, positioning her butt on the back of the armchair. "Spread your legs."

Her thighs were wet with her own juices, glistening in the dark. This only seemed to ignite him. The second she did as told, he pressed up against her, his hard prick rubbing against her wet folds.

Both of them wanted it and they would get it, but not before he had confirmed one last thing.

"Tell me, what do you feel for me." He suddenly demanded, halting all actions. "Say it and your debt will be forgotten." His voice grew more demanding when she didn't respond right away.

"I...can't explain it. I don't know if I can trust you, but I can't resist...I want you, but not just sex. You're the biggest jerk I know. You're arrogant and filthy rich. I detest people like you and yet....I can't stay away." She whispered, all her emotions pouring into the words. "I need to know....can I trust you? Or will you betray me."

"I won't betray you." He murmured, his hand that wasn't holding her waist traveling up to caress her thick hair. "I am many things, most of them bad. I can't blame you for not trusting me. But...I wouldn't betray the woman I love."

Catherine sucked in a deep breath, pure happiness lightening her eyes. Her lips crashed into his passionately. He returned the kiss, groaning into it. One of his hands traveled underneath her knee, lifting it to his waist before he thrust into her with a swift move.

His hips pounded against her own, their kiss interrupted by lustful moans from both parties. Nothing could stop the moment of bliss and steamy sex. He made her feel like she was in heaven, each thrust reaching deeply inside her.

Layton's other hand reached for her other leg, wrapping both of them around him as he carried on, his breath resting against her neck.

He held her orgasm hostage a couple of times, but when it came, it came crushing down on her like a wave. Catherine threw her head back and did not bother to keep her voice quiet. Her scream echoed through the suite, followed by his deep growls as he released the white gunk across her flat stomach moments later.

It wasn't enough, however.

They had to have more.

When they were done, sun had begun to peek over the horizon. Both of them had somehow ended up in the bed, exhausted. She laid besides him, her cheek put snugly against his wide chest and her arm dangling over his torso.

The day followed by their ravenous activities had her dead. She couldn't move or even keep her eyes open. A small smile played on her lips as she sunk into deep sleep.

"Catherine." Layton's voice sounded distant, just barely keeping her from falling unconscious. All she could respond with was a silent 'hm?'.

"Do you realize how your life will change now?"

Catherine grunted. He had the best sense of time for serious questions.

"You can no longer live like you used to, if you chose to stay with me. There are many people craving my power or loathing me for who I am. I deleted my mother's memories because they put her in danger. I want to give you a choice, and you have to think very carefully about it."

Catherine forced her eyes to peel open, looking up at him. Layton was gently playing with her hair, his eyes holding something she hadn't seen in them before. Warmth.

"What are the options?"

"Stay with me and turn your life upside down. You will be put in danger, even if I will protect you, they will still come for you, specially when your soul awakes in a couple of days. If you chose to go down this route, your life will never be....no rmal." He explained, the warmth sinking behind emotionless gaze. "The other option; I will delete your memories-"

"No!"

"Hear me out." Layton said strictly, leaving no space for objection. "I will ensure that you are well situated. Every month, I will send you a certain sum of money, just enough for you to live well. You will have a chance at normal life...a family."

"I already made my decision." Catherine was interrupted by a feather kiss on her lips.

"No, I want you to think seriously about this. A month from now, I will ask you the answer, only then I will be sure that you've made your decision." He caressed her cheek. "Do we have a deal?"

She did not like the sound of this, but she did not object. He was right and it was only fair that he gave her this choice. Catherine nodded. "Deal."

Epilogue

1 MONTH LATER.

"And that's it?"

"Yup."

"I don't feel anything."

"You're not supposed to. Only creatures with power, like me, can feel the change. Your scent is different."

"How boring. I was expecting something more dramatic like flashes of light or...or...wings! I was hoping for wings!"

"Don't be so childish."

A little less than a month had passed since her soul 'changed'. She had expected something big to happen, but instead the night was spend on Layton's couch with a bowl of chips and Netflix. The most shocking thing was Layton liking Stranger Things.

Honestly, she had no idea what the buzz was about until much later.

It was no lie about the attacks. After their chill night, all hell broke lose. Three attacks in three weeks, all coming from different demons. Layton had become overprotective. She barely talked him out of buying her a bulletproof vest and basically turning her into cheap version of FBI agent.

Being looked at like a five course meal was certainly one of the most annoying things. The sight of Victoria licking her lips when she walked inside the room never failed to give Catherine creeps. Thank God she hadn't met the rest of the family during the time. She'd be gobbled up in an instant.

Specially by that Gluttony guy...

Perhaps she couldn't feel it, but things did change, and manly because she was with Layton. Many wanted him dead or suffering and she was his weakness.

I wouldn't say I'm his girlfriend...He is not the 'label' guy. But what am I? Sex buddy? Closest thing to friend in his life? His lover?He said he loves me only once...A girl deserves to hear it more...

"Catherine."

At least he calls me by my first name.

"Catherine!"

She was shaken from her thoughts with a deep voice cutting through the inner monologue. Blinking, she found herself standing in middle of a meeting room with a couple pairs of eyes boring into her.

One pair in particular got all of her attention.

"Have you quit gawking at a wall and I can get my coffee? Or that's too much to ask?" Layton was giving her his infamous glare. He sat in his usual place at the end of the table, his arms set on the wooden surface and his imposing figure leaned forwards slightly.

There were five more men in the room, much older than the CEO himself. All of them wore tailored suits that cost fortune and frowns as if it was a part of the formal attire.

"It's so hard to find a good assistant these days. All of them are slow-minded. At least you have one that's nice to look at." One of them commented, ugly grin plastered on his old face.

Catherine frowned. She was pretty used to people talking about her like she wasn't even there and in most cases, she didn't care, but this was just annoying.

A part of her considered dumping the coffee on the old man's lap.

"This one is pretty decent when she's not spacing out." Layton grumbled, his attention now on papers laid out in front of him.

Pretty decent!?

Catherine gave her lover a dark look, setting his coffee onto the table. "Here's your coffee, sir." The platter she used to carry the coffee was purposely bumped against the back of his head, just enough to making him look up at her.

"Anything else?" She smiled innocently at the blue eyed man, ignoring how annoyed he looked.

Somethings never change...

"No. You may leave." Layton waved her off, but just as she was about to exit the meeting room, he spoke again. "Just don't forget that this is an important night."

Catherine froze up with her hand hovering above the door knob. She had completely forgotten. Today marked one month since they made the deal and she was ought to give her answer today...

Glancing over her shoulder, she gave a brief nod before rushing out. She had been so confident in his arms, feeling safe and protected. Layton even kept his promise, he did not take her soul or harm her. But she also knew the reality of remaining by his side. It will be a life full with danger, demons lurking on every corner.

This was honestly the biggest decision she was to make.

I have fallen in love with the worst man possible....my god damn luck...

Long sigh escaped her lips as she sauntered back to her office.

The hours dragged and no amount of work could ease the building tension. Most of the time she just flat out stared at the computer screen. The evening hadn't even come and she nearly had a heart attack twice, all thanks to Jeremy, Victoria's assistant that had come by with a question or two.

Layton was in meetings all day. This was an important time for the company - or at least that's what he said.

She couldn't get over the feeling that he was avoiding her.

When the clock hit 8 pm, she couldn't take it anymore.

"That's it." Catherine stood up from her chair, the tension raising to it's peak.

I can't take this anymore.

She marched to Layton's office, swinging the door open. "Layton! We have to tal-Huh?"

Catherine was met with an empty office chair. His scheduled meetings were over an hour ago, but he was nowhere in sight.

"He's really avoiding me." She murmured, glaring at the desk that was always littered by documents, and this time, something else as well. Her eyebrows furrowed. There was a letter with her name and red rose set onto his closed laptop.

The handwriting was like someone had wrote with a chicken leg. She had thought her handwriting was bad, until she had seen Layton's. There was no mistaking that monstrosity for anyone else's.

The letter contained three simple words: Follow the roses.

This left her even more confused than before.

Since when is he romantic? Is he plotting something?

Terribly suspicious, and slightly disturbed, Catherine walked out from the office with the letter and the blood red rose in hand. Couple steps in, she found another one laying by the elevator. Most people had already gone home at this point, leaving her alone to wander around.

The trail carried on until she reached the bottom floor where a driver was waiting for her at the front door.

"Miss Cavenon. Mr. Grim is expecting you." The man spoke, handing her the third rose and opening the door for her.

Catherine could only picture how awkward that looked from third point perspective. A fancy driver in a fancy suit holding open the door of a fancy car, for a girl in old sneakers and skinny jeans.

She had screwed the dress code long ago.

"Thanks?" Catherine gave him a wry smile.

Like, really!? What the fuck is he plotting!?

The driver gently closed the door behind her. The man had patience like ocean, he never told her to hurry up and she had hesitated quite a bit.

On the backseat was a large box with another rose and a letter.

"Wear this?" She read, growing seriously puzzled. Inside the box was a pretty knee-length dress and a pair of matching black heels. "Am I supposed to change here!?"

"Yes, Miss. Do not worry, I won't be looking." The driver responded politely, pressing a button that lifted a sort of a wall between her and the front of the car. Yet another fancy detail she was no used to.

The drive was not long, but boy, was it a struggle. By the time the car halted, her cheeks had gone red with the effort put into changing her clothes in a moving vehicle. It wasn't as easy as movies made it seem for sure!

They had stopped in front of a five star restaurant. Angelique had bragged about this place and how it was hard to book a table there. She had said something about a line six months in advance. Catherine could only stand and gawk at the beautiful glass entrance, decorated by countless little lights to give it a romantic feel.

This was not the local Burger King she was used to.

Two waiters escorted her inside and the first thing she saw was the culprit of this whole mess himself.

"You look...acceptable." Layton spoke, his eyes skimming over her. "I see you ditched your shoes again."

"Can you not be a jerk for once? And I am not going to wear those killer shoes, thank you." Catherine grumbled, slightly uncomfortable under his intense gaze.

He smirked, "I just prefer you with no clothes on."

"Pervert." The young woman fought not to blush, even more that is. Somehow his words always got to her. "What is this place anyway? A Ghost town?" Aside from the staff, they were the only ones in the restaurant. All tables were empty.

"I reserved this place for us."

"That's insane!" Catherine felt her jaw drop. Only this man would be capable of something like that.

"Not if you're rich." Layton shrugged casually, leading her to one of the tables. Two glasses of wine were set onto the table near empty plates. The waiter brought them the first course the second the two were seated.

The food looked strange. She was too ashamed to ask what the small thing on her plate was, but it certainly wasn't enough to soothe her hunger. With her being nervous, she had completely forgotten about lunch.

"So, umm? What is this for?" Catherine asked hesitantly, for a second ripping her attention away from the food. God knows, it took effort.

"I wanted privacy for both of us." Layton spoke, sipping on his red wine. "Did you like the roses?"

"I did! But, you didn't have to."

"I wanted to. I promised not to interfere with you decision, but I couldn't resist." He set the glass down, his attention now fully on her. "There are things you should know before you tell me your answer."

"Layton...I already made my decision."

"No. You should hear this before you make the final answer." He insisted. "First, if I erase your memories, I won't be able to return them. You won't remember anything that has happened since you jumped in front of my car."

"I did not do that! You were driving way above speed limit with your eyes closed!" Catherine interjected, earning herself a pointed glare, which she ignored. "I don't want to hear all this."

"You have to know what's on the table here."

"I know that already!"

"No-" Layton was cut off by napkin being flung at him.

"Will you shut the fuck up and listen to me for once!?" Catherine seethed. She had enough of all the details about her memories being deleted, when she didn't want it in the first place. "I don't want you to do anything! I want to stay with you and I don't give a shit about demons and sins or whatever. My life has never been normal. Period."

Silence settled among the two. And then, the most unimaginable thing happened.

Layton smiled.

He didn't smirk or grin. He smiled. A genuine smile that exposed charming dimples at the corners of his mouth.

In a blink, he was up from his seat and standing by her side. Catherine didn't get to add anything before she was scooped up into his strong arms. She gasped as he spun her around, hugging her tightly like she would poof into the air any moment.

Never had she seen him act like this. A child getting his favorite toy for Christmas was the closest thing she could describe the emotion that was running through him. It was pure joy.

When he finally set her down on her feet, both of his arms settled on her waist. "I was hoping you would say that." He whispered, the boyish smile still on his lips. "Catherine..." Her name sounded sweet rolling off of his tongue. He said it so delicately and gently that it made her heart melt.

"You're mine now. All of you."

"I would like to hang onto my soul." Catherine chuckled, leaning into him. The world was lost. It was only the two of them.

"I want to make it official." Layton said after a moment of brief, happy silence. He had turned serious again, gazing into her eyes. "I want you to merry me."

Her eyes widened. "Wait...what?"

"Be my wife."

As if someone had turned her on mute, Catherine was speechless. She could only watch as Layton sunk down on his one knee in front of her.

"There is no turning back from the decision you made, I hope you realize that. So, I want you to become mine in all ways possible." He produced a small ring from his pocket, large diamond shining in the dim light of the restaurant.

"Where....is the camera? Are you trying to prank me?" Catherine glanced around, but there was only the two of them.

"No. I am serious. What is your answer?" He asked, growing impatient.

An evil part of her wanted to torture him and savor the moment a tad longer. A sin, kneeling before her....

But the answer came shortly.

"Yes." She choked out, watching Layton slip the ring onto her finger. He looked relieved, but soon it all faded back to that infamous grin.

"Finally, I can do whatever I want with you." He stood up, his sadistic side coming through the warmth.

"On the second hand, keep the ring-" She was silenced by their lips locking into a deep, passionate kiss. It stole the breath from her lungs. Each soft caress made her crave more of his touch. It didn't last as long as she wished it to. Layton pulled back, resting his forehead against hers.

"Too late. You're my fiancee." He closed his arms around her. "There's no escaping me now, spitfire."

Catherine smirked. "And there's no getting rid of me, Mr. Sin."

Her life had never been easy. It was never meant to be simple either. But who would've guessed that a poor girl would once become a sin's bride?

It was one hell of a journey...and something told her, that it had just begun.

www.ingramcontent.com/pod-product-compliance
Lightning Source LLC
Chambersburg PA
CBHW070938190726
48292CB00004B/1225